Mafia Premier League

Dr K. Vijayakarthikeyan is an award-winning and bestselling author. Two of his novels—*Once Upon an IAS Exam* and *Heartquake*—were extremely popular and remained on AC Nielsen's prestigious weekly National Bestseller Book Ratings list for multiple weeks. Both these books were acclaimed for their breezy charm, sharp wit and sprightly narratives, and will soon be aired as web series. He also received the Most Inspiring Author Award at the Gurgaon Literature Festival. The young doctor-turned-bureaucrat, who is as popular for his enthralling fiction as his engaging non-fiction books, has so far published 10 books in English and Tamil.

Also by the author:

Once Upon an IAS Exam
Heartquake

Mafia Premier League

K. VIJAYAKARTHIKEYAN

RUPA

Published by
Rupa Publications India Pvt. Ltd 2021
7/16, Ansari Road, Daryaganj
New Delhi 110002

Sales centres:
Allahabad Bengaluru Chennai
Hyderabad Jaipur Kathmandu
Kolkata Mumbai

Copyright © K. Vijayakarthikeyan 2021

All rights reserved.

No part of this publication may be reproduced, transmitted, or stored in a retrieval system, in any form or by any means, electronic, mechanical, photocopying, recording or otherwise, without the prior permission of the publisher.

This is a work of fiction. Names, characters, places and incidents are either the product of the author's imagination or are used fictitiously and any resemblance to any actual person, living or dead, events or locales is entirely coincidental.

ISBN: 978-93-91256-31-9

First impression 2021

10 9 8 7 6 5 4 3 2 1

The moral right of the author has been asserted.

Printed at HT Media Ltd, Greater Noida

This book is sold subject to the condition that it shall not, by way of trade or otherwise, be lent, resold, hired out, or otherwise circulated, without the publisher's prior consent, in any form of binding or cover other than that in which it is published.

Contents

1. Reunion — 1
2. Coffee, Chocolates and Coke — 10
3. Dosa and the Dragons — 19
4. Tale of Questions — 27
5. The Full Circle — 35
6. Friends and Foes — 43
7. Yesterdays and Tomorrows — 51
8. Balls and Bullets — 60
9. Twists and Turns — 69
10. Threads and Notes — 78
11. Bid-ridden — 87
12. A Tale of Three Hospitals — 98
13. Building Blocks — 107
14. Insights — 115
15. Dragon Wars — 124
16. Missing Pieces — 135
17. Final Strokes — 141
18. Hot Pursuit — 151
19. Reunion 2.0 — 160

CHAPTER 1

Reunion

'Thousand rupees, from Nerul to Dongri? Green Taxi costs only seven hundred! This is nightlight robbery!' cribbed Ricky as he took out the money from his pocket.

'Then go in Green Taxi next time!' quipped a gleeful driver as he almost snatched the money from Ricky's hand and drove away.

'Is that still Mr Malhotra's beach house?' Ricky asked a passer-by.

'Which Malhotra?' the man asked, without breaking his walk.

'Textilewala… the big magnate!'

The passer-by's facial expression changed completely as Ricky mentioned those words. Ricky could literally read fear in the man's eyes. His whole body shook and trembled. He changed direction, turned his back to Ricky and walked away without uttering a single word.

Though Ricky had been to this place before, he felt unsure. A lot had changed and he didn't want any trouble. All the wounds inside him were still fresh.

Ricky then took out his phone and dialled a number.

'Hi Pravi, Ricky here.'

'Ricky!'

After that there was complete silence from Pravi's end.

'Hello! Pravi?' Ricky spoke in a soft and caring tone.

Pravi took deep breaths. This was the first time she had heard from Ricky in years. A few years ago, they were really good friends and Pravi had a crush on Ricky. Just when she started showing feelings for him, an unfortunate turn of events forced Ricky to go underground. She tried contacting him, but in vain.

And now here he was, after three years! His voice brought back so many memories. Pravi tried controlling her emotions and pretended to be normal.

'You back in town?'

'Yuppity! I'm near the beach house, though not sure if things are still the same.'

Oh! Beach house huh! Things have never been better. And now that you are here, it's the icing on the cake.'

'Are you there now?'

'Nope! I'm at the cinema.'

'Can we meet tomorrow around noon for coffee?'

It was all surreal for Pravi. She pretended as if she was looking at her schedule and slowly replied in a carefully constructed, listless tone, 'Okay.'

∽

Ricky walked towards the location shared by Pravi. As he approached the place, he started hearing deafening music. 'MM type music indeed,' thought Ricky as he took the left. There was an array of cars parked haphazardly along the path leading to the dead end. The dead end was the opening into MM's 'den', as he would call it. *'Laila Main Laila'* was playing at the highest decibel possible as Ricky entered the place. The heavy pounding of the music kept increasing as Ricky walked towards the front door.

Before Ricky could turn the handle and open the door, the door opened and a couple of young women with a hyperbolized coat of make-up and 'hypobolized' sets of skimpy clothes opened the door and walked past him. Ricky went in to see multiple versions of the women who had just gone past him. 'Aah! Familiar sights, sounds and fragrances,' exclaimed Ricky as he walked into the foyer.

'Drink your hearts out!' burst out a fat figure sitting by the piano, in the darkest corner of the foyer.

'He has been sitting with the piano for a long time. Does he even play it?' asked a confused guest to a blurry eyed neighbour.

'He always sits by the piano in all his parties. Once I even asked him if he plays it.'

'Oh! Did you? And what was his reply?'

'He said, "sitting like this is classy hain na? Then, why bother playing? Big shots sit like this only, haven't you seen in movies?" And started laughing!

I couldn't ask more because he is MM! One more question and he might just take out his gun and shoot me. With MM you never know what's cooking or what's coming!'

True! With MM one never knew what was cooking or coming. Max Malhotra was drinking his eighth glass of the night. A short and burly guy, weighing well above 100 kilos and just entering his 50s, MM was the stereotypical self-made, rags-to-riches Mumbai guy. Raised in the choked neighbourhoods of Dongri, he had worked with Karim Aziz, a textile merchant, throughout his teens. After a decade of working with Aziz, they had a fallout which led him to set up his own business.

Malhotra always wanted the maximum out of everything. Be

it efforts, money or a share in the trade. He gave his maximum and always wanted the 'Max' back. He worked hard and rose on the financial and social ladder. Within a few years' time, he had established an array of textile manufacturing units to go with his chain of outlets. His obsession with being a 'Max' person made him bring all his business units under the umbrella of MM industries—short for 'Max' Malhotra. In short, he was the 'Max of all Trades'!

Max of everything also meant unreasonable targets and dreams. This was when MM went from white to grey to the darkest of black! Drugs, prostitution, money laundering… MM was into everything. Every item on the underworld's menu was in MM's pocket. As MM's network grew, he connected with the who's who of Mumbai's underworld and the choicest of international smugglers and traffickers. And as he grew, he also got earmarked by the police and soon became one of their prime targets in Mumbai. After almost two decades of cat and mouse games with the police, MM got caught in a mid-sea shoot-out operation, based on a tip off about a deal, three years ago. This broke MM's backbone and sent shivers through the Mumbai underworld.

Though MM was the brains behind all his operations, he did not carry out any of the activities himself. And so, the Mumbai police were hardly able to produce any evidence against MM in court. Several of his accomplices, in fact, came forward and took all the blame, matching themselves with the evidence and exhibits presented in the court, without revealing anything about MM's role in any of the crimes.

The Mumbai police tried their best to hold MM, citing interrogation and also seeking time to procure more evidence. They could keep him for one-and-a-half years in Arthur Road prison, but couldn't succeed beyond that. A combination of lack of concrete evidence, high-powered lawyers and MM's super influential network got him released. After his release, MM was perceived by many to have dumped all his illegal activities and to have gone back solely to his textile life. Many within and outside his network found it hard to believe what they saw and felt MM was only doing it to evade the surveillance of law enforcement agencies. He believed MM getting back to action was just a matter of time.

It was at this time, much to everyone's surprise, that MM hit an unexpected 'sixer' and purchased a cricket team in the Mumbai Super League, popularly called the MSL. 'Classy, isn't it? To own a cricket team?' he told whomever he met. 'Being classy' was the other obsession that MM had, which he also believed to be true about himself, much to the disappointment and, at times, disgust of others.

'Drink as much as you want! We have a cricket team now. MM bhai is celebrating tonight. When MM bhai celebrates, the entire town celebrates,' declared Billu, pausing the music briefly.

Billu was MM's side, front and back kick. Billu had been with MM ever since MM opened his first textile shop. Well into his 40s, Billu, unlike MM, was a tall and strong guy. His prized possessions were his goatee and his chiselled body. They were also the only things that he really cared about. Billu had always been a part of MM's legal, illegal and extra-legal plans.

At times, MM was foolish with his words, sometimes even on purpose, just to let people underestimate him. He was otherwise a shrewd guy with sharp, calculative moves, which were always a step ahead of that of his rivals. Billu, on the other hand, was always foolish with his words, thoughts and actions. He was mostly seen trumpeting MM's greatness and beating up people on MM's orders. In the famous shoot-out, Billu had also been arrested along with MM.

Ricky briefly browsed through the foyer as he walked towards the piano. MM was gleefully accepting compliments from a few cops. Guests, many of whom Ricky recognised to be a part of MM's network, were having a gala time, celebrating their old friend's new-found love for the gentleman's game.

'Rickeee,' screamed MM as he saw him walk towards the piano.

'How are you man, how long it's been!' cried MM as he hugged Ricky across the piano with difficulty.

'Three years and two months, MM bhai,' Ricky said, in an emotional tone.

'You scoundrel, you came to Mumbai a few days back, yet you found time to meet me only now?'

'Haha! How did you know?'

'MM knows everything! I also know that you are meeting Pravi for coffee tomorrow!'

'Rameez had sent a small consignment for delivery, bhai. Was working on that. Came straight here once that job was done!'

'Hamesha, work comes first for you. *Hain na*? You are still the same! Come come, it's noisy here, let's go to the other room.' MM held Ricky's hand and took him to the other room. Ricky was almost as tall and muscular as Billu, with a shock of dyed red hair, clean shaven all the time and was just about to enter his 40s. The only difference between Billu and Ricky was that Ricky was not foolish. He was sensible and shrewd enough to run MM's affairs smoothly. In short, Ricky had the brawn that MM never had, and the brain that Billu never had, which was why in a short span of time, he had become MM's prized associate. During the mid-sea shoot-out, Ricky was badly injured in the cross-fire but managed a miraculous escape.

'Haven't heard a word about you since that wretched day. When Rameez told me that you were working for him, I immediately sent word for you!'

'Yeah, MM bhai! I took two shots to my body from Zia's gun on that bloody day. Somehow managed to pull a raft and fell into the water. I don't know what happened after that. I was later told that some fisherfolk took me to the shore and also got me admitted in a missionary hospital. I regained consciousness at the hospital and tried to reach you. But soon found out that you were arrested and the entire network was shut. Thought I'll also shut shop and keep a low profile until things became normal. So, I flew to Dubai and worked at a supermarket. Completely stayed away from the grass or powder market.'

'Hehehe! Supermarket?! The most feared hitman of Mumbai working in a supermarket. How classy is that?' laughed MM.

'I know it wasn't. I was deeply frustrated too. But wanted to be off the radar and safe. I was sure that Zia was gunning for me. All she wanted was a tip off for my rip off!'

'Don't utter that name. My blood boils. I had to rot in jail for more than a year because of her. Lost my network. Lost my throne. I will design her end. Don't worry!' hissed MM.

'We will, MM bhai. I was fortunate to stumble upon Rameez bhai a few months back in Abu Dhabi. After all, Dongri has roots all over the world! Worked for Rameez bhai for a few months. Rameez bhai had a decent powder network in Abu Dhabi. He sent me to Goa to deliver a consignment. As I finished delivering the consignment, Rameez bhai told me that you had sent word for me. I immediately knew things had cleared up. So, I came to see you but never expected this from you, bhai,' said Ricky.

'Expected what?' asked MM in an intrigued tone, as his phone rang. As MM was speaking on the phone, a huge glass box placed at the corner of the living room caught Ricky's attention. It was a transparent box, made of toughened glass, inside which three hens were pecking around.

'Expected what?' MM asked Ricky again.

'This cricket team, bhai. Remember once you had asked me the difference between a four and a six in cricket. Why would you buy a team now? Why this new passion suddenly?' quizzed Ricky.

'Hehehe! You know what. There is more to the game than just bat and balls. That is what jail has taught me!'

'Jail teaches something new to everyone who goes inside. But still, cricket for you is totally flummoxing! Were you with some match-fixing convict in the cell, bhai? You still think there are good returns for match fixing in a city-based league? I doubt we have a viable betting market to feed into city level fixing. We may have to wait for such a betting market to gain momentum, MM bhai.'

'*Arey bachaa*! Match fixing, spot fixing, these are just a fraction of the action. You wait and watch the main action! Our team is going to be the epicentre of all the action!'

'So, under the guise of a cricket team owner, you are going to restart our network! I get it now, MM bhai!' Ricky sounded relieved and happy.

'Not just restarting the network. There is much more! Much more than you could ever imagine! I will take care of all that. I will also be the face of the team. It will help in cleaning up my image. You just run the actual cricketing operations of the team. I will take care of everything else. And watch out for a sixer!' roared MM, a laugh full of vengeance and confidence.

He walked across the room to a chamber close to the glass box and pulled a lever. There was a sudden loud sound in the glass box. The loitering hens gave a death cry and kept beating against the box, trying to escape. The sound grew louder and suddenly, with a huge thud, a six-foot black-headed python emerged out of the rocks. It advanced steadily towards the hens whose primal cries drowned out the loud music that was playing. Their attempts to escape were in vain, as the python clutched them one-by-one with ease, crushed and swallowed them all in one go. It then came to the edge of the box, turned towards MM and hissed loudly. MM bent to the level of the snake box and planted a kiss on the glass, superimposing his lips on his pet's head, with only the glass separating them.

'Old habits die hard,' sighed Ricky.

CHAPTER 2

Coffee, Chocolates and Coke

Three years ago
Maharishi Apartments, Lower Parel, Mumbai

'A good conversation
Bit of ogling at you
A selfie
And a warm hug.
That's all I need.'

Vivank smiled reading the text on his Twitter chat from @Leepa323. 'See you at 7 p.m., then. You choose a place,' replied Vivank, with a smiley and got into his shower.

Vivank Sharma was one of the most prominent names in the Indian domestic cricket circuit. The 35-year-old was once touted to be the next big thing in Indian cricket. His blistering century in just 43 balls, during his Ranji debut for Mumbai, against Rajasthan made eye balls pop. He was a young 20-year-old lad then. He became an overnight superstar in Mumbai cricketing circles and went on to score tonnes of runs for Mumbai throughout the 2000–01 season, with his aggressive brand of batting.

'Did you watch the news? Virender just got selected to the Indian test team. Your batting style is so similar to his. One day I'm sure you will be like him,' his childhood coach would encourage him. Vivank continued his rich vein of form for the next few years and made a mark for himself in the Mumbai limited overs and test team. There were even talks of an Indian team call-up and Vivank's stakes were at an all-time high. His happy-go-lucky nature won him a lot of friends and his growing stature in the cricketing circuit increased his fan following.

Ever so strong on the field, Vivank's brilliant delivery soon came off the field in the form of illegal cocaine, which his 'new social group' had introduced him to. 'Snort one more line, just one more line,' they would urge him until he was completely out of control. Practice sessions, team meetings, yoga and pool sessions—Vivank started missing everything. His sprint timings took a beating and fitness standards fell to an all-time low.

'I know what you are up to. Better mend your ways or else you are going straight out of the team. You know very well what it took to get to where you are now. You will go nowhere like this,' warned Havalkar, the head coach of the Mumbai cricket team. However hard Vivank tried, he couldn't let go off his dangerous new habit and that led to a horrible dip in his batting form. Havalkar, true to his words, dropped Vivank from the team in 2004 and from the squad in 2005.

This was a huge blow for someone like Vivank who had always believed that he was gifted and great things were in store for him. Everything happened before he could even blink.

'Nothing! You are nothing without that bat in your hand. Wake up at least now. Go back to your innate habits and restart your cricketing routine,' said Cheeku with utmost anger.

Vivank's parents were doctors and were working in Singapore. Vivank stayed in India only to pursue his cricketing dreams. Cheeku was Vivank's best friend since college days and one of the few true friends Vivank had. Cheeku, though a software engineer by profession, was an ardent cricket follower and had brilliant insight into the game. He hired a personal trainer-cum-coach for Vivank and put him on a tough regimen to restart his cricketing career.

Cheeku's arrangement had a telling effect on Vivank, as he started rediscovering his lost mojo with the bat and his fitness. He was back, playing for Mumbai in 2008 and also won himself a decent contract with Real Madras—the Chennai based franchise. This was in the inaugural edition of the nation's premier T20 league—The Indian Cricket Blast. He had an amazing run for the franchise as well as for Mumbai until 2012, when he once again went back to his coke ways. All the advice that his cricketing friends and Cheeku gave him amounted to nothing. Vivank lost his way and toppled out of the cricketing radar yet again.

'How many times will you put me through this? Do I deserve this? Why do I even need your friendship? How many times will you betray us? Every time we believe that you will achieve bigger things, you end up disappointing us. Why should your parents slog in a foreign country while you happily go about doing coke here? Just go away and leave all of us alone!' An angry and disappointed Cheeku vented out.

'I'm trying my best to let go, just that I get carried away at times,' replied Vivank, in a helpless tone.

'If I see that Rodriguez once again with you, I'll take both of you to the police. Have you heard of DCP Zia? She will smack you so hard that you will leave everything behind and run to your parents in Singapore. Your poor parents who still think that you will become a Mahendra Singh Dhoni will then know who you really are! That will indeed be a happy sight for me to watch, considering the things that you make me go through,' Cheeku poured out in disgust.

'Okay. Give me one last chance. I will try my best. I don't have anything more to say,' begged Vivank.

However much he tried, Cheeku could never give up on Vivank.

'This is your last chance. Don't make a fool out of me and yourself again,' replied Cheeku.

Vivank started his comeback drills all over again. He was the butt of all the jokes and trolls among the cricket pundits. 'All he does is make comebacks,' laughed a commentator on air during the Indian Cricket Blast. 'Play. Dope. Comeback. Repeat.'—read a meme with Vivank's picture, which went viral on social media. Vivank was deeply frustrated seeing all this but was also determined more than ever to make a mark. Although he was 32 already, he was still hopeful of playing for India one day. He put his best foot forward the next couple of years, worked hard on his game and started getting some good scores, but his consistency was missing. His fitness also was failing him, as the deadly aftereffects of coke started taking a toll on his body.

He would be scoring 20 plus runs off the first 8–10 balls he faced and would then throw his wicket away. That element of greatness in his game, which was there 12–13 years back was somehow missing now. But Vivank stuck to his basics, kept fighting his inner demons and kept himself afloat. He tried to contribute as much as he could to the team. With age catching up with him, his hopes of playing for India were rapidly diminishing by the day.

Vivank never had as deep a connection with women, as he

had with cricket and coke. Just a few casual relationships here and there was all he had ever experienced.

'Cricket, coke before girls,' he would casually tell Cheeku.

'Saaale, coke, coke and only coke for you. Nothing else you care about! *Chup karo!*' Cheeku would retort strongly.

Vivank was on one of his causal Twitter chats when he started receiving texts from @Leepa323. As he opened his DM box, he noticed that he had been receiving messages from this handle for almost four years now. He then started to chat and soon discovered it was a girl who claimed to be his fan.

Upon chatting with her for the next few days, he realised that the girl really liked him and decided to give it a shot. She wanted to meet him that day and he agreed to meet her at 7 p.m., at a place of her choice.

'Café Truckso is okay with you?' Vivank saw the text as he came out of the shower.

Vivank reached Café Truckso exactly as the clock struck seven. It was a truck themed coffee-shop where chairs, tables, mugs and every other piece of utensil and furniture was designed as a truck. Vivank climbed up the stairs and sat on the most colourful truck by the window, looking out over the Arabian Sea. Soon he saw a tall, slim and extremely fair woman walking towards him. Dressed in a grey round neck t-shirt and blue jeans, a fitness watch and floral flip-flops, the woman walked briskly towards Vivank with her sling sports bag wrapped over her left shoulder.

'Hi, I'm Leepa. Leepa Azam,' she held her hand out and firmly shook Vivank's hand.

'Sorry, I'm late by five minutes. I've been waiting for this moment for a long time,' she continued with a blush, taking her truck seat.

'Fourth floor in Maharishi Apartment, right? Flat facing the park. My gym is right across. I stop and wait there for a few minutes daily, near your balcony, hoping to catch a glimpse of you,' she continued as the blush deepened.

'So, you saw me while commuting to your gym?' asked Vivank sheepishly.

'No, I found a gym close to your place, so that I could travel there daily.'

'But why didn't you talk to me sooner?'

'Why didn't you check your messages sooner? The only better thing I could have done was ringing your house bell. Had I done that, I'm sure I would have only bumped into that Cheeku of yours,' said Leepa brimming with happiness.

'How do you know Cheeku?'

'Your own Instagram profile has more pictures of him than yours. Plus, he tags you in all his posts. Almost every day I see him loitering around your house. The other day I saw him hanging wet clothes on the balcony for drying and in the next two minutes he posts "#WeekendsBelike #ViewFromMyRoom", with some photoshopped picture from Helsinki and tagged you. I have seen more of him than you, actually!'

Vivank started laughing even before Leepa could complete her sentence. Vivank showed her his phone. Cheeku had just uploaded yet another picture tagged "#ViewFromMyRoom #WeekendsBeLike" from Budapest.

'Then surely your friend must be drying clothes in the balcony,' said Leepa as they both burst into a prolonged bout of laughter.

'Tall, extremely thin, with that unshaved beard and your "capsicum" like nose! You are just how I had always seen you, known you and imagined you,' said Leepa.

'Haha! "Capsicum" nose, those are the exact words that my mother used to say!' said a visibly chuffed Vivank. 'Why did your parents name you Leepa? Is that even your real name?'

'Of course, that's my real name! My ammi named me after our home town Leepa. When I was born, she thought that I was the most beautiful person on earth and there was no greater word to describe me than the most beautiful Leepa Valley where I was born,' she replied.

'Where is it?' Vivank asked.

'It's in Kashmir. About 80 km from Muzaffarabad. Such a beautiful place, a real paradise! I wish to take you there one day,' Leepa said with a mix of pride and love.

'Very nice! Your family still lives there?'

'No, we moved out during the Kargil War when I was about eight years old. My father works for the Mumbai water board, my mother is a homemaker.'

'What about you?' Vivank asked

'I work at Imperial Bank. Elphinstone Road branch. I'm the branch manager there.'

'But you don't look like a banker!'

'You too don't look like a professional cricketer!'

Both shared hearty laughter.

Their chatter and laughter went on for the next couple of hours with shots of espresso until Vivank got a call.

Vivank picked up the call even before he could stop laughing.

'What? Have you started with coke again? Where are you?' It was Cheeku.

'No no! I'm out with a friend,' replied Vivank.

'Who, Rodriguez? I'm coming there now with the police,' Cheeku got to his warning ways.

'Shut up, you fool. I'll be home in 30 minutes,' Vivank hung up.

'Guess it's time to go. Selfie?' asked a starry-eyed Leepa.

'One selfie is never one selfie,' is the popular saying. Vivank and Leepa ended with about 120 shots in a span of five minutes.

'I'm gonna post it with the Eiffel Tower in the backdrop and tag your Cheeku...' Before Leepa could complete the joke, Vivank fulfilled her wish by pulling her towards him and giving her a warm hug.

Leepa pulled out Vivank's favourite brand of chocolates from her bag and gave him.

'I won't even ask how you know these are my favourite chocolates,' smiled Vivank. Leepa shook her head and smiled back.

They rung the truck honk hard at the exit and went home, still smiling!

Present day
Café Truckso

'Never thought I'd see you again,' said Pravi, sipping coffee and looking straight into Ricky's eyes.

'I always thought I'd see you again. I just wanted to wait out the dark period. That's why I didn't try getting in touch with any of you until the coast was clear,' smiled Ricky.

The two fed each other with their three-year stories and shared their emotions.

'You have been very brave, I must say!' complimented Ricky. 'Stuck it out with MM during the difficult times,' he continued.

'That, I have always done with MM. Will continue to do forever. After all, he has given me everything in life.'

'Do you have a girlfriend?' Pravi asked, hoping and praying for a 'No'.

'I'm too old for all that! Isn't it?'

'Yes, and I knew you would say this! You are known for your escapist answers!' Pravi laughed.

'Are you going to stick with MM?' she asked.

'Of course! The moment I heard from Rameez bhai that MM was back on his feet, I decided that I would get back. And I was gratified to hear that MM was actually looking for me.

And like MM, I too have scores to settle! And revenges to accomplish. However much bloody they turn out to be.' His tone had changed suddenly. He had become emotional. 'And to answer you straight, YES! I'm going to stick with MM till the very end.'

Pravi held his hand and comforted him.

'Hey, I know you well Ricky. I know how you feel even now. MM and I talked it through so many times. Now is not the right time. Let's concentrate on the things at hand.'

'Like what? Take the cricket bat and run around?'

'In life, each phase is a challenge and each phase has to be dealt with differently. A wait today is a win tomorrow! Remember!' said Pravi.

'A wait today is a win tomorrow! Nice lines. You are becoming a pro at this, Pravi,' said Ricky.

'I'm a pro at whatever I do,' smiled Pravi.

'Come let's take a selfie. It's been a long time,' she added.

CHAPTER 3

Dosa and the Dragons

Three years ago
Maharishi Apartments, Lower Parel

'Is that girl a drug peddler? Or is she high on powder or weed always?' Cheeku asked.

'Is that a joke?' Vivank asked, looking pissed.

'Come on bro, you know it.'

'She's a good girl and I like her. That's what I am trying to convey.'

'Like how you liked the other women so far?!' Cheeku didn't want to give up without having his kill.

'Did I want to go out with them daily or have I even discussed them with you'? asked Vivank.

'Hmm. I'm good with it as long as it's not dope!' replied Cheeku.

'Well! Thank you for your approval, I got to get going now. Meeting her for breakfast!

By the way, don't Instagram while drying your clothes in the balcony. You are being trolled, laughed at and ridiculed!'

'Wow! I love South Indian food! How did you know?' exclaimed Leepa, as she got out of the car.

'Well, let's just say social media is for everyone!' smiled Vivank.

In less than 24 hours, Leepa and Vivank had become so close to each other and felt they were made for each other. They shared a lot of common interests like travel, food, cricket. Both had a good sense of humour and were extremely impulsive. Both loved dosa too!

'It was very sweet of you to have picked me up from home. We met last night for the first time. Here we are, together again, for breakfast!' Leepa couldn't hide her excitement as they walked into Madras Bhavan.

'One ghee dosa for me,' said Vivank.

'Plain dosa for me,' Leepa decided and placed the orders.

'How come you are eating such stuff, despite being a professional cricketer. Isn't stuff like ghee dosa, biriyani and paranthas restricted?'

'Haha! I have done worse things. Ghee dosa must be the last thing on the worry list!' Vivank gave a frank reply.

'Hmm, I too have read. Been following your news all these days. You should have been dominating world cricket by now. I, as a fan, feel so frustrated seeing the way things are. Can't even imagine being you,' Leepa's tone was truly empathetic.

'Certain things are out of my control. Whatever happens, happens. I've learnt to take things in my stride. I should just try to stay on the radar and be a better person with every passing day,' Vivank replied in deep philosophical tone.

'Yeah! All said and done you have never given up. I love that about you!' Leepa reiterated her feelings.

'Thank you! Feels so good that somebody still has faith in me.

By the way what is that 323 in your social media handle? That @leepa323,' asked Vivank curiously.

'That's your highest first-class score, buddhu! Scored against Punjab, in the 2002 Ranji trophy semi-finals,' Leepa said proudly.

'Oh my god! That's amazing. I should really thank my stars for having met you,' Vivank couldn't hide his amazement.

'Looks like the boy has been swept off his feet, for a change!' winked Leepa taking a bite into her dosa.

'Not just swept. Reverse swept!'

'That was just a sample. I have collected all your newspaper cuttings, videos, interviews and everything about you. I created your Wikipedia page, FYI.'

Vivank held her hands and kissed them.

Happy tears rolled down Leepa's eyes as they looked deeply into each other's eyes.

'You must be the first person on earth to have given a sambar kiss! Sambar that was in my hands is now on your lips!' Leepa had a 'teary' laugh.

'I love you, Leepa,' Vivank confessed, wiping the sambar away.

'I love you more, Vivank,' said Leepa, stamping her love over him.

'Well, matches were made in heaven once, then in coffee shops and now in dosa shops it seems!' laughed Vivank.

'That is a PJ. I'm sure you have borrowed this line from Cheeku!'

They both laughed in unison, yet again at the cost of Cheeku.

'You don't worry about anything. Just focus on your game. I'm there with you. Will be there with you,' Leepa spoke in an assuring tone.

'Mom and Dad will be thrilled to meet you. I'm so happy.

Can't wait to watch you all meet.' Vivank was now visibly excited.

'I can't wait for that too! I'm so so excited, Vivank.'

'What about your parents?' asked Vivank

'They asked me a thousand questions before I got into that car with you today. Did you notice their faces as we started? They may not like this at all. But frankly I don't care about that. I have always done what they wanted me to do, now is the time for me to do what I really wish to do. No one is going to stop me!' said Leepa. 'But don't worry. I will never bring all those pressures to you. Those are my issues. I will handle them myself. You be free… just see the ball and "chakka maar",' she quickly added.

'We met yesterday for the first time. Look at us now! In less than 24 hours, we have proposed to each other and are discussing meeting the parents! Well, I mean…er… that's kinda too fast for even my scoring rate! Which fool would do that?' Vivank expressed in happy disbelief.

'Yeah! But that's beautiful right?'

'True. I know it's a hasty decision that we have made. But it's a decision taken from the bottom of our hearts and we are like this. So, let's just continue to be like this always!' said Vivank. 'This feeling that I'm getting now is priceless. I have never experienced anything like this before,' he continued.

'Hello mister! I bloody created your Wikipedia page! I have all the data including your horoscope with me! I don't care about all that. I still love you wholeheartedly,' said Leepa with abundant love and kissed Vivank.

'And I will ensure that our love only grows by the day,' said Vivank, holding Leepa's sambar-free, clean hands for the first time. 'This isn't even love at first sight! This is love at first bite!' he said.

'Haha! Another CJ…Cheeku joke,' Leepa laughed and fell into

Vivank's arms and the two were lost in each other for the next few minutes.

'When is the season starting? What are your prospects?' Leepa asked, sitting up.

'It's starting this August, on the 23rd. I'm in the team, and will surely start most of the games. At 34, I don't have many expectations. I just need to help the team win as many matches as possible and help out with the upcoming youngsters. That's what I'm looking at,' replied Vivank.

'Well! All the best! My love and prayers will always be with you!' said Leepa.

'Don't make a wish immediately as if we won't meet for the next one month. I'll be surprised if we don't meet again for dinner tonight,' Vivank quickly replied.

They laughed in unison as they got in Vivank's car.

Present day
A 5-star Hotel in Powai

'What's this party about?' a loitering guest asked Billu gulping down his whiskey.

'Fool! Don't you know? MM has bought a team for the inaugural edition of the Mumbai Super League.'

'Well, how many times would you celebrate that? I saw you all drinking and dancing in Dongri last week!' replied the guest.

'That was for buying a cricket team in the Mumbai Super League,' replied Billu.

'Am I making sense?' the guest asked his friend who was party to the entire conversation.

'Yes yes! You are talking sense. This guy doesn't seem to get it!' said the friend.

'Oye Billu! I'm asking one last time. Why are they having a party now?'

'I'm telling you again. MM has bought a team in the upcoming MSL! We are celebrating that,' replied Billu.

The two drunken men who were goons themselves picked up bottles and almost got into a brawl with Billu.

'This party is for the official announcement of the team's name,' said Pravi, as she took Billu away, rather forcibly.

Some 25 years ago, MM had picked up an abandoned girl child, from the gullies of Dongri and raised her as his own giving her the name Pravi Malhotra. As much as he continued to annoy her, by trying to give her some classy 'lifestyle hacks' almost daily, he took good care of her as he would have done if he had a daughter of his own. As she grew up, Pravi started helping MM in his work and eventually, efficiently ran his 'legitimate' businesses. In fact, it was Pravi who managed all of MM's legitimate businesses and wealth when MM was in jail and when most of his associates too were either in jail or in hiding. With a post-graduation degree in business administration, Pravi was by far the most educated person in MM's circle! She was about 28 now, fair, short in terms of her hair cut and height! Headstrong and opinionated, she always had a chewing gum in her mouth, which she would spit out in case she disagreed with something being said. Pravi was well trained in karate, kung fu and taekwondo.

'I will blow your face away the next time you speak foolishly and start trouble,' she warned Billu before letting him go.

Ricky and MM were busy discussing something as the crowd that had gathered to listen to the announcement was getting impatient.

'Is this a sarkari function which never starts or ends on time?' they joked.

Finally, MM went on stage with his glittering 'team owner'-type tuxedo and pulled out a card.

'DONGRI DRAGONS' the card read.

There was a huge round of applause along with confetti and coloured flower showers and over-the-top firework animations on a giant screen fixed behind the stage.

'At this stage, as the chairman of Dongri Dragons Sports Limited, I would nominate Ms Pravi as the managing director and Mr Ricky as the chief operating officer,' MM announced.

Pravi was visibly pleased and felt proud. Ricky kept a stone face and managed a brief smile.

For Ricky, who always had larger priorities and vengeful ambitions, a cricket team's COO wasn't a big deal. It took a lot of convincing from MM and Pravi to get him to accept the job.

'My third and final announcement for the night is that Dongri Dragons Sports Limited has also acquired RKM Residential School, Uttam Hill. The school ground will serve as the home ground for Dongri Dragons during this year's MSL,' MM added.

'First a cricket team and now a school. This is a new MM we are seeing. Will he ever get back to old ways?' There was a huge buzz within his network.

'Dongri Dragons! What a classy name!' MM was boasting to Ricky over a glass of Dom Pérignon.

'How did you come up with this name, MM bhai?' asked Ricky.

'Game of Thrones. From Khaleesi and her dragons. I have always felt that I'm a male version of Khaleesi! Only the dragons were missing and here they are now!' he proclaimed.

Present day
Somewhere near the Mumbai port

'No sir! People like Ahmed Shah are very elusive and beyond our reach! Taking him down, will require a super cop and a super team on a blood hunt. I'm neither a super cop nor do I have a super team.' It was DCP Zia talking to one of her political bosses.

'I know you have him. Let him go immediately,' warned the voice from the other side.

'Extremely sorry, sir. As much as I would love to have him in custody, I have to admit my failure at this point, sir,' Zia answered over the phone as she watched the video stream from MM's event.

'You have been telling me the same thing to me for half an hour now. Where are you now? I will come there,' said the voice angrily.

'Sorry sir! I'm on leave. I'm in Goa with my family, sir. Sir… sir…unable to hear you, sir…bad signal, sir…sir…'

Zia hung up and flung the phone towards one of the constables who was standing nearby, for a catch, which the constable missed.

'Saala, you dropped this. How will you catch a thief?'

'Dongri Dragons! What is this fool up to now?' remarked Inspector Rathod, pointing at the video.

'He never was nor will ever be a fool. MM is one of the most cunning and thorough criminals I have ever seen,' Zia remarked.

'Let him begin his game, ma'am. If we sense any mischief, we will nab him straightaway!' said a fiery Rathod.

'No more nabbing! Aim at the forehead, two inches above the glabella and shoot,' Zia remarked, cool as ever.

Right at the corner of the room, tied to a chair surrounded by a pool of blood was Ahmed Shah. Cold and motionless with rigor mortis setting in slowly. Ahmed's eyes still reflected the pain and torture that he had undergone. Right on his forehead, two inches above the glabella was a huge bullet mark.

CHAPTER 4

Tale of Questions

Two years ago
Blue Paradise Beach Resort, Panjim, Goa

The alarm went off at 6 a.m.

Vivank reluctantly got out of his cosy quilt, shutting off the alarm. He stretched a bit and went to the window, still half asleep. As he drew the curtains, the sun slowly emerged from the waters, kissing everything on its way out.

'Hey! Let me sleep for some more time,' cried Leepa from underneath the quilt in the laziest of tones.

'Just open your eyes for two minutes, then you can go back to your sleep!' Vivank persuaded her and pulled her out of the bed, went behind her and shut her eyes with his hands and took her towards the window. Vivank then slowly withdrew his hands from Leepa's eyes. Leepa opened her eyes with a smile to see the sun kissing her a good morning! Her happiness was instantly elevated by the kiss Vivank planted on her cheeks and her forehead. He then brought her back to the comforts of her quilt and said, 'Now sleep as much as you want! I have to get ready and attend practice.'

Vivank was in Goa to play the Mumbai–Goa state trophy tie that was to happen the next day. Vivank and Leepa had been together for about a year now and she would travel with him to almost all his away matches. As wives and girlfriends were strictly forbidden to stay with the team, Vivank made an excuse every time and stayed out with Leepa. As he himself used to say, his chances of playing for India were almost nil. He had a contract with the Mumbai team for another couple of years. His contract with the Indian Cricket Blast franchise, Real Madras was due to end this season, and as such Vivank was dropped from a few games in the previous seasons of the lucrative T20 league. Even when he got to play, he lost his preferred batting position at the top of the order to younger players. Vivank was having a decent domestic season, but he needed something extraordinary to keep his T20 contract with Real Madras.

The headache was absolutely throbbing. It was as if all his nerve endings and joints stood together inside his skull and were slamming down with a sledge hammer. Vivank also felt tremors and palpitations. It had been almost a year since he was off dope before he started again a month ago due to performance anxiety and depression over his cricketing future. He was on and off the powder for a month now, resulting in intense mood swings and the physical effects that he felt right now.

A part of him was dying to lay hands on coke, yet another part was killing him with guilt. Guilt of lying to Leepa about abstinence from coke and thereby cheating her, guilt of betraying his parents and Cheeku, guilt of screwing up his own career, guilt of ruining his dreams. Everything put together as a cocktail was crushing Vivank. It was as if his head was going to explode any moment now.

Vivank went through his drills at the Porvorim Cricket ground with all this in mind. At the end of the session, the Mumbai captain confirmed that Vivank would feature in the playing 11 of the next day's match. Since they would be playing the next morning, they decided to call off the evening practice session and rest. In the context of the domestic league, it was a must win game for Mumbai to stay afloat in its bid to qualify to the next stage of the competition.

'Hey Vivank! With great difficulty I fixed up a seller for you. And you don't respond to my calls. What do you think of yourself?' It was Rodriguez yelling at the other end.

'With the kind of client base that I have, I should not even be following you this much. I'm only doing this because you're an old friend,' he continued in the same tone.

'I'm not sure if I would need them now, Rodri,' replied a confused Vivank.

'Who will pay all my dues then, you oaf,' Rodriguez's started raising his pitch.

'In a couple of hours I will send you a location near Mapusa market. Go there and call me. My person will meet you to collect the dues. If you are not there on time, my person will come directly to your room—Vivank Sharma, 108, Blue Paradise Resort,' Rodriguez gave his ultimatum.

Now this was another tonne of baggage placed over his existing mental load.

Leepa was still lying where he had left her.

Same place. Same posture. Same sleep.

She woke up and hugged him when she realised he was back.

'Let's eat something and go to the beach. I haven't eaten anything since last night,' said Leepa.

'Okay.' Vivank was too preoccupied to say anything else.

And that 'Okay' was enough for Leepa to understand that something was wrong.

'You don't seem to be your usual self. Are you not well or something? Or is there an issue? Please tell me. I'm there for you always,' Leepa spoke reassuringly, taking in a spoonful of Goan fish curry and rice.

'No nothing! Headache that's all.' Vivank didn't want Leepa to think less of him. More than opening up to Leepa, he was worried about managing Rodriguez.

'I think I know what's bothering you. Are they sitting you out of tomorrow's game? I know that young kid, Shreyas, is playing awesome but nobody can be like you. You are the best,' Leepa was as faithful and supportive as ever.

Soon they were walking by the beach adjacent to their resort.

'Let's ride a water scooter!' Leepa cried with excitement.

'Yeah sure,' said Vivank and he set out to pay and hire a water scooter.

The water scooter ride was an amazing experience for Leepa. 'I've never done this before. It's super fun,' she was literally screaming.

Wonderful weather, crystal clear water, with his dream girl behind him, water scooter in full throttle—this should have been the ride of his life. Unfortunately, for Vivank, it wasn't to be the case.

'Will Rodriguez send his person to our resort? What will happen if I don't pay up? Why is it that a part of me still wants dope?' All these jumbled thoughts were running through his mind, as he and Leepa zoomed through the waves deep into the ocean.

'That was out of the world! I thoroughly enjoyed it,' Leepa still couldn't get over the awesomeness of the ride.

'Yeah yeah,' nodded Vivank without even processing Leepa's comment.

'Give me your shirt. It's drenched. Let me dry it for you,' Leepa held her hands out to get his shirt.

Vivank gave it to her and went to return their water scooter to the shop.

The evening was gorgeous and dusk was slowly approaching. Vivank got back to where he had left Leepa but she wasn't there. Vivank's heart started pounding. He realised that he had left his phone in his shirt pocket. Grief-stricken, he hopelessly looked around for Leepa. Unable to find her, he started running frantically to their room.

The door was open. He could hear Leepa crying. His pounding heart was in unison with Leepa's blubbering.

For a year, they had been laughing in unison but now suddenly, their pain, their agony, their affliction was all in unison.

'You lied to me! You betrayed me! You cheated me!' She kept crying out loud as she stuffed her things quickly into her bag and packed them.

That furious look she gave Vivank as he started to explain made him shut up and watch her helplessly, as she packed her bags.

'Here!' Throwing the phone in his face, she said 'it's over. Now and forever.' She slammed the door and walked away from Vivank.

Vivank knew that once Leepa made up her mind about something, no amount of convincing would help change her decision. Her decisions were drastic but always firm. Nothing could change that. Not even his love. She had given him her everything but he had ruined it all.

Vivank stood numb. The weight and pressure on his head were immeasurable. His limbs started to tremor, eye balls began to get pulled inward, his throat was getting choked, he couldn't breathe. Vivank fell with a loud thud and a violent bout of seizures.

Present day
DCP Office, Mumbai

Zia was sitting and playing Candy Crush on her phone. With every candy that was being crushed, she was thinking about crushing MM and his network.

'Good evening, ma'am,' wished Inspector Rathod promptly as he entered Zia's room along with another person in civil dress.

Both customarily saluted Zia and stood in front of her.

'So, Rathod ji what's the progress?' asked Zia.

'Just came out of the HUMINT wing, ma'am. Had a detailed discussion with the intelligence team. This is Inspector Himanshu. DC Intelligence has deputed Himanshu Saab for our assignment ma'am,' briefed Rathod.

'So, tell me Himanshu ji. How are the surveillance activities progressing? I have received a tip-off that MM is planning something massively nefarious. We have every reason to believe that he will be back to his old ways. We let him off the hook once. It should not happen again. We should pounce on him even before he can think of escaping,' Zia said.

'Yes, ma'am. We have deployed some high-end multilateration techniques to track his and his close aides' movements from signals picked up from their mobile phones. We are also looking to wiretap their phones. MM uses a completely encrypted phone, we are trying our best to decrypt it,' reported Himanshu.

There was a beep on Zia's landline. She picked it up.

'Ma'am we have traced the call records from all their mobile operators and have emailed you a summarised report,' said the voice at the other end.

Zia opened her iPad and looked into the summarised report.

'So many calls made abroad in the last 10 days. Have international cricketers been allowed to play MSL?' Zia remarked sarcastically. 'If he is making calls to international numbers, I'm sure there must be some data sent through mails and other forms. To what extent can we get into that?' asked Zia.

'We have hacked a few such channels already, ma'am. No major yield,' replied Rathod.

'There could be some steganographic techniques being used. Did you look for or try to break them?' Zia asked.

'Steganographic?' asked a perplexed Rathod.

'It's the practice of concealing a file or a message or an image within another file, message or image,' Zia replied.

She knows all this but sits with Candy Crush, Rathod thought to himself, as he nodded away religiously to Zia's explanation.

'We did, ma'am. We will look more carefully now,' replied Rathod.

'Don't give such sarkari-type answers! You have either looked into it or you haven't.

This type of answer will get us nowhere,' Zia replied irritably.

'Sorry, ma'am,' replied a confused Rathod.

'Also, take a detailed look into MM industries' financial dealings, fund transfers and any change in clientele base. Get inputs from the Directorate of Revenue Intelligence and prepare a consolidated report for me, ASAP,' Zia shot out the orders loud and clear.

Zia had always been a shooter. She either shot people without caring about orders at the other end or shot orders without caring about people at the other end! Either way, she always had her way, in whatever she undertook.

'You both can go now. Stay alert and look out for any clues, small or big. And don't forget to intimate everything to me ASAP,' she shot again.

'Yes, ma'am!' said both the inspectors as they left the room.

It was around 1 a.m. and Zia had just started to prepare her dinner. She was in her early 30s, extremely tall, fair and skinny. Highly ambitious and widely regarded as one of the most courageous and daring officers around, Zia lived alone in her apartment in Kandivali. Rumour had it, that she had been in a live-in relationship with a guy, but the relationship couldn't last because of her temperament.

Zia had always wanted to be the best and worked tirelessly and to the best of her ability.

Zia's phone rang at 1.30 a.m. It was Inspector Himanshu at the other end.

'Looking at MM related transactions and based on the inputs obtained from the Directorate of Revenue Intelligence, it seems MM has transferred a lot of money to an unidentifiable Chinese firm in the last one week. We are trying to trace the backend information regarding the details of the firm. But no concrete info yet on the firm, ma'am,' reported Himanshu sincerely.

'How much has been transferred?' asked Zia.

'About ₹50 crore in small, multiple batches in the last one week alone, ma'am!'

'Oh!'

Zia hung up the phone looking perplexed. *'What is MM up to now? Why is he making aberrated payments to an unknown Chinese firm? What next?'* Every candy in the game looked like a question to her as she continued playing.

CHAPTER 5

The Full Circle

Present day
Maharishi Apartments, Lower Parel, Mumbai

'Leepa Azam' Vivank typed out his daily search query on all his social media handles.

'I am still blocked from all her accounts. This is unfair, yaar,' complained Vivank.

'You think everyone will be as gullible and foolish as me?' Cheeku was at his cheekiest.

'Even I would have left you if not for your parents. Just imagine the shock that you gave them in Goa. They literally dropped everything and ran to be by your side. They just kept sitting and praying outside the ICU for a month and then were waiting and praying as you went through your full course of rehabilitation. For almost two years they have been patiently living their life for you and have left just last week, handing you over to me. I'm still sticking by you purely because of the love and respect I have for your parents,' Cheeku ranted breathlessly.

'So, you don't respect me?' Vivank asked after a long pause.

'You? Who will respect you? Your loyal fan and faithful

girlfriend kicked you out! And rightfully so!' answered Cheeku.

Vivank remained silent. He had spoken enough all through his life. Promised all his life. Defending himself for the wrong things and unable to preserve the right things. He didn't want to talk or promise anything to anyone, anymore.

His phone rang suddenly.

Truecaller said L.A and showed the callers category as banking!

Vivank's heart started pounding again. With trembling fingers, he received the call.

'Good afternoon, sir.' Vivank realised it wasn't Leepa.

'We are calling from Bank of Hindustan. There is now a super attractive home loan offer. Would you…' Vivank yelled at her and hung up.

'What's wrong with you? Why are you mad and yelling at people?' Cheeku tried to reason, as if he did not know.

'Yeah! What good reason do I have to be mad?! My relationship ended two years now. I don't even know if I'll ever have a relationship again.

My dream career is over! Whatever I wanted to achieve, I clearly did not!

My reputation is far away from me, farther than the longest sixer I've ever hit.

And I'm called a fucking drug addict.

You ask me what's wrong with me? What more could ever go wrong for anybody? Powder! Girlfriend gone and also career gone. What a loser!' Vivank finished all he had to say at one go.

Before Cheeku could start, 'Now please shut up. I'm in no mood for your divine interventions and discourses. Get back to Instagram,' shouted Vivank.

During the last two years, Vivank had even contemplated ending his life on more than one occasion. But it was this lingering anger in him, building up a firewall, that prevented him from committing another foolish act. Vivank, since then, had been wilfully cultivating this anger. Vivank started believing that because he was so easy on himself, life decided to be tough on him. He was determined to change that. He was ready for this role reversal in life. If only it would give him another chance.

'Will it?' He was desperately hoping and praying in the guise of thinking.

'Whatever could have gone wrong has gone wrong. What more can happen now?' Suddenly he dared life with his new-found anger.

His phone rang.

Vivank looked at the screen, put the phone down and placed both his hands on his head without uttering anything.

Cheeku came and picked up the phone. The caller name read Rodriguez!

Cheeku gave him that same deadly look that Leepa had given Vivank before she had left him.

'No! Rodriguez has nothing to do with me anymore. I'm sure. I have settled everything. It's done and dusted. I haven't spoken to him for a long time now,' Vivank literally pleaded.

Rodriguez called again.

'One more time you call this number, you will be in jail and on YouTube,' Cheeku picked up the call and threatened Rodriguez.

'Jail is okay. No YouTube, bro!' Rodriguez replied.

'Did I sound like I was offering you choices? Now hang up before I block you,' warned Cheeku.

'No…no…wait. I want to meet Vivank,' Rodriguez quickly uttered.

'Do one thing. Come home with a knife and slit his throat.

You are anyways going to be in jail for a long time,' replied an angry Cheeku.

'No…no, it's something else. I can explain in person. It's for his good only. I will be there in one hour,' replied Rodriguez.

'You better bring the knife too,' answered Cheeku and hung up.

∞

Rodriguez was a dwarf in his late 30s. He used to work in a snack bar right outside Vivank's college and had known him since his college days. Three things defined Rodriguez physically. First, of course, was his height. Second was his curled-up hair and third, were the tattoos all over his body. Literally every inch of his skin was covered in tattoos. Apart from these, only one other thing defined him. Money! He was someone who would do anything for that one word. That was his only ideology and his tongue would wag in any direction to accommodate his ideology.

'Hey Vivank! Wassup dude?' he called out as he entered the living room of Vivank's apartment.

Neither Vivank nor Cheeku responded.

'Sorry dude! My mistake. Whatever has happened, has happened. I have not come here to talk dope,' Rodriguez spoke in a reassuring tone.

'Then? What else do you want from me? My kidneys? Only those are left now! You are into that racket too?!' This was the 'new' Vivank speaking now.

'Hey! Hey! You speak to me as though I am a criminal!'

'No! No!' You are the president of the United States.'

'Fine! I thought I too was morally responsible for whatever happened to you. You may not believe me but I too felt the guilt. Then there came an opportunity to redeem things. Thought I'd talk to you about it,' Rodriguez said.

'What is it?' Cheeku interjected.

'You've heard about MSL? Mumbai Super League? Dongri Dragons, a team owned by the textile baron MM is looking for a coach.' Rodriguez was speaking as Cheeku and Vivank looked at each other.

'What's your cut in this?' Cheeku asked

'How does that even bother you. Of course, there's money in it for me. But money isn't the only thing in this. I can get rid of my guilt too,' Rodriguez said.

'You are friends with MM?' Cheeku was looking for details.

'I'm friends with Billu, one of MM's inner circle guys. He is one of my main suppliers. He will connect me to the managing director of the team, Ms Pravi Malhotra. Of course, there will be a selection process, but I think Vivank will get through,' said Rodriguez.

'Your supplier's supplier! Vivank's prospective employer! How prestigious!' Cheeku exuded sarcasm but he was really unsure.

'It's not about that. For two years I have been without opportunity. Finally, something has come my way. What I couldn't achieve as a player, I could try to achieve as a coach. I know nothing other than cricket. This is essentially the only way I can take my life forward,' Vivank spoke as if he had made up his mind already.

'I'm still not sure. I don't want any more nonsense. This MM-Vivank-Rodriguez connection is not inspiring. It seems like a tailor-made team for a drug racket just waiting to be busted,' Cheeku started laughing aloud thinking about the combo.

I will come, Rody! Just tell me when and where!' Vivank said in a bold tone.

Vivank was on his way to the new office of Dongri Dragons Cricket Limited. Scenes of everything that had happened to him so far in his life played like a slideshow in his mind. He had one opportunity to rewrite some parts of that life and right a few of his wrongs. *'This could well be my last opportunity,'* he thought as his taxi approached the office. He had been through the utmost humiliation after the Goa episode. He was unceremoniously sacked from both the Mumbai team and his franchise team, and the press portrayed him as if he was the most dangerous creature to have walked the earth. The aftereffects of it were so bad that his Mumbai coach Havalkar, his franchise coach and most of his friends from the cricket circle stopped talking to him. The cricket board almost banned him before he provided adequate medical proof that he wasn't on drugs at the time he collapsed in the hotel.

'Cricketer Vivank Sharma found dead in hotel room following a cocaine overdose' flashed as the first breaking news that day! Vivank had lived through all that and more and was still living. Living to redeem himself. Living to have another shot at life!

'Sorry! You are rejected.' Pravi didn't even look at his CV or give him an opportunity to talk. Billu, who had taken him to her, tried to explain but she wouldn't listen. She plainly showed Vivank the door!

Yet another humiliation for Vivank. He didn't know what to do or say. When Pravi rejected him, he only felt anger. Anger at his own self. He said to himself that he deserved it fully.

'You are Vivank Sharma aren't you?' asked a voice from atop the stairs. It was Ricky.

'Yes,' Vivank answered clearing his throat.

'He has come to apply for the coach's role,' Billu said.

'Then why is he standing there? Ask him to come up to my

room,' said Ricky as he walked in.

'Vivank Sharma is the best possible coach we could get. Unless you could talk to someone by the name of Sachin Tendulkar,' Ricky was talking to Pravi over the phone as Vivank and Billu sat in front of him.

'Ricky is the COO of the team,' Billu whispered to Vivank.

Ricky had always had his way with Pravi. No matter what. That was primarily because Pravi had always had feelings for Ricky. No matter how adamant she was, she always gave in to Ricky.

'If I had been denied the opportunity by MM five years ago, I would be a nobody. Same goes for everyone else here. Don't judge people by their past,' Ricky was pulling all his weight.

'See, I understand all that. But why get into unnecessary controversy when we have easier options. At the time of crisis, you went off to Dubai. It was me who pulled everything together and ran the show,' Pravi was giving in, yet she was spelling out justifications.

'You have easier choices but do you have better choices?' asked Ricky.

'That I'm not sure,' came the reply.

'On numerous occasions I have paid to watch this guy play. He is damn good. He will deliver,' said Ricky.

Tears rolled down Vivank's face.

Pravi closed her eyes and thought for a second. She herself had risen from the streets, literally. She had given second chances to quite a few people in her life. And if Ricky was backing someone, he ought to be worthy, more often than not.

'Okay. Fine. You have your way as always!' Pravi hung up reluctantly.

'Congratulations! You are the coach of the Dongri Dragons cricket team,' announced Ricky.

'Thank you, sir, from the bottom of my heart. I will never forget your help,' replied an emotional Vivank.

'I have followed you enough to know how good you are. Not just the skill set, you have a very sharp cricketing brain too. I still remember the last ball you played against the Delhi team during the Cricket Blast final a couple of years ago. Two runs needed off the last ball, opposition placed all their fielders on the boundary, you cheekily tapped the ball close, ran two runs and won the game. That street smart Vivank is what we need for the Dragons,' said Ricky.

Vivank had goosebumps by the time Ricky had finished talking.

'Sure sir, I will give it my all,' Vivank nodded and got up, thanking Ricky again.

'And just two more things. First, no more "sir" to address me. Ricky should be good. And second and most importantly, no more dope!' Ricky emphasized clearly.

'Yes, sir. I would rather die, than touch dope again. Thank you for everything,' replied a confident Vivank.

Vivank walked out of the office with a new-found pride. A pride which he wanted to keep all his life. He was now ready to give everything to the game. The game he loved more than anything. The beast in him was awake!

CHAPTER 6

Friends and Foes

Present day
Cheeku's office, Bandra West

'One day we will meet again
And you will teach me
How to fall in love again…'

Vivank liked that 'quotable quote' on FB, still thinking about Leepa as he waited for Cheeku, who was apparently in some meeting.

The beast in him was awake but the beautiful flowers and butterflies in his heart, which had been in paradise a few years ago were crushed and surrounded by darkness and empty space now. On the one hand, he was happy that he could still salvage a career out of cricket. On the other hand, he was thinking about Leepa. The emptiness her exit had caused in his life.

Even now, his brain was divided. Cricket occupied one half. Leepa occupied the other. Dope fortunately had vanished since his rehab.

'How has she gone so long without talking to me? Has she moved on? Is she married now?'

The thought of her marrying somebody else caused an unbearable pain in his heart.

'How did it go?'

Cheeku came out after an hour to meet Vivank.

Vivank gave him a thumbs-up sign.

'Powder or weed? What do they want you to sell? How much is your brokerage?' Cheeku asked with a chuckle.

'Cricket coach. That too after a lot of scrutiny and humiliation. I deserve it though,' Vivank started to narrate his interview story.

Cheeku took him to his office food-court to continue their talk.

'I simply couldn't sit at home and wait for you. I wanted to know what you think and get started. I'm tired of sitting at home, doing nothing. And the more I think of Leepa, the more I long for her and the more I'm hurt. I want to break this cycle,' Vivank poured his heart out to Cheeku.

'What if you start doping again?' Cheeku asked. Now, Cheeku was the one pouring his heart out.

Vivank felt like slapping Cheeku. He would have done it if it had been somebody else.

'No point being angry with me,' Cheeku spoke knowing what Vivank was thinking.

'Now what do you want? I'm going ahead with this assignment. If you don't trust me, you also come with me! Leave your work!' Vivank was furious.

'That is exactly what I'm gonna do, beta,' Cheeku spoke in a zen like tone.

'What?!' Vivank couldn't believe what he was hearing.

'I mean, I will be with you until I feel you are good enough to be left alone!' he clarified.

'What about your job here? And who will employ you there?

I had to beg so much,' asked a confused Vivank.

Frankly, Vivank didn't know how to react. He didn't like this baby-sitting attitude, but he wanted to be back in the game at any cost and Cheeku was, after all, his best friend.

'Your entire work schedule will be around three months, starting with the player auction next month. Before that there is a one-month window to scout players. As you would have known by now, MSL allows four outstation players per squad and two in the playing 11. I can be the team scout and analyst. I can just take leave here for a month or two. I'm anyway a data analyst here and I understand the game as much as you do,' Cheeku spoke without a pause.

Vivank gave him a death-stare.

'Okay, you understand the game better. It is just that I can help you better. In fact, help you better than anyone else.'

'For a moment you spoke as if you had won the previous cricket world cup with team India! You really think that they are waiting for you to join them and unearth the next Dhoni?' Vivank asked maintaining the stare.

'You don't have to worry about that, bhai! Rody called me as soon as your thing was confirmed. He then helped me connect with Ricky. This Ricky seems good. He sounded optimistic too. I'm awaiting confirmation any moment now.' Cheeku clean-bowled Vivank with his words.

'What about your job here?' Vivank still couldn't believe what he was hearing. He was shocked as well as surprised but was also happy deep inside.

'I told you...I'll take leave for a month or two. Fortunately, unlike you, my reputation here is very good. You would have sensed it by now by seeing the "likes" and "comments" I get on my Instagram posts.'

The phone rang. 'Haan, Rody tell me!' Cheeku answered the call.

'So, this Rody and Cheeku are friends now! How funny life is,' Vivank thought to himself.

'I'm on board buddy. Team scout-cum-data analyst. Will have to report to the head coach Vivank Sharma it seems,' Cheeku declared happily.

'Report later. Now, go scout for some Channa samosas, I'm very hungry,' declared Vivank.

∽

DCP Office, Mumbai

Zia was becoming extremely impatient. Her upgraded Candy Crush version was getting stuck while downloading. She couldn't figure a way out and was desperately trying to set it right. On the other hand, her quest to nab MM was also stuck without a way forward. She was desperately thinking of a way to set that right.

'Good evening, ma'am!' the duo of Rathod and Himanshu reported in unison.

'What's the progress?' she asked in a slightly frustrated tone.

'We have found out the name of the Chinese firm to which MM industries transferred ₹50 crore last week. It's called the Red Moon Corporation, it's an infrastructure company,' replied Rathod.

'Yeah. Received your text regarding that. I had also asked you both to track down all the items listed to be shipped to India from Red Moon Corporation, either delivered last week or to be delivered in the coming 1–3 weeks. Also to take the help and inputs from customs stationed at the port. Did you do that?' Zia asked, hoping for a breakthrough.

'Yes, ma'am. Working on that. We will be able to track it only once it reaches the Indian shores. I have also put in a word to the air cargo base. Hopefully something will come up ma'am,' Himanshu replied diligently.

As much Zia looked the cool daredevil on the outside, she was an extremely frustrated soul, always cribbing on the inside. She felt like slapping both the men in order to vent out her frustration. Zia felt her own inability to crack down this alleged masterplan by MM would reduce her to being a loser. She had almost reached the pinnacle of her frustration, but resumed her discussion with a calm face.

'That's fine. These things take time. Don't panic. Don't worry. We will definitely get to the bottom of this.'

'One more piece of important information, ma'am,' Himanshu spoke in a low tone.

'What is it?' Zia asked

'A group of 10–12 foreign nationals who are linked to drug dealing and drug related crimes across the globe are meeting with MM in a week's time,' Himanshu said in a hushed tone.

'Oh! I was waiting for something like this! You should have told me this first! You first eat your dessert, then your food, and finally drink the soup, huh?' Zia's happy sarcasm was making its way out. 'Are you sure about this?' she asked using her cool-cop tone.

'Yes, ma'am. More than one source has confirmed this,' Himanshu replied confidently.

'We could believe "sources" if we were one of those newspapers or news channels that carry front page headlines about massive scandals without verification. Given our situation don't you think we should wait for confirmation?' Zia was thinking aloud.

'It's better to confirm and cross-check before proceeding,

ma'am,' Rathod voiced his opinion first, having been a long-time colleague of Zia and a part of most of her operations.

'Even on the day of the shoot-out at sea, we waited until we got a confirmation about the deal that was happening and only then proceeded,' Rathod reminded Zia.

'That's also the reason they got to use that extra bit of time and got rid of most of their evidence,' Zia reminded Rathod.

'Yes, ma'am. Then let's go all out. We will not spare them this time,' said Rathod in a rogue tone.

'Okay. Intensify the surveillance then. We don't know the place yet but having known MM well, he would prefer the sea or some place near it where he could quickly get away by water in case things go south. Also try to get information regarding the timing as quickly as possible. We are getting a large company this time and we can take them out once and for all,' Zia was brimming with enthusiasm as she uttered those words. She had joined the police force only for days such as these and was truly living it up.

Suddenly her mood changed drastically—from frustration to excitement! Her phone beeped to tell her that her Candy Crush update was complete and was ready to play!

'Yeah, baby! Ready to play! Bring it on!' She picked up her phone.

∽

Same night
MM's residence, Powai

MM was playing teen-patti with Ricky and Billu, sitting at a billiards table in his living room. The entire house was dimly lit and silent. There was a huge glass chamber in this house as well. The red headed python, for a change, was sitting on the branch of a small artificial tree that MM had gotten custom-made for his pet. The python was hissing restlessly, waiting for food.

The doorbell rang. One of MM's men answered the bell.

Inspector Rathod was standing there with a sheepish smile.

'Oye, Ricky. When did you come back?' He happily patted Ricky's back and sat by the billiards table.

'Bhai, if I ask you why you are playing teen patti on a billiards table you will definitely say it's classy,' Rathod remarked, with a sense of pride that he could guess MM's reactions.

'Is it not true? Inspector Rathod!' replied MM as he picked up a card.

'Bhai, I have something important to report,' started Rathod.

'As if I didn't know. Otherwise, why would you come without me asking you to. Now out with it quickly. I want to play,' urged MM.

'Bhai, Zia knows about the dealers meeting. And she is making big plans to trap you and finish you off along with the entire gang,' Rathod gave MM and company a 'loyal' warning.

'Hahaha!' MM gave an orchestrated, loud and ugly laugh, sipping whiskey.

'She thinks herself to be an intelligent daredevil, right? Let her plan, let her plan,' MM sounded arrogantly confident about the situation.

Rathod looked completely perplexed at MM's cool attitude. Rathod at least expected an 'Oh! thanks for alerting'-type reply from MM, instead he was almost trolled by MM.

'Don't be careless, bhai. Zia almost brought all of you down once,' Rathod sounded his second 'goodwill' warning.

'Do you really think it was Himanshu who became Ethan Hunt and got this info?' MM laughed.

'Then?' Rathod was more confused now.

'I wanted Zia and Himanshu to know about it. So, I planted it in a way that the news would reach them. In other words, it was a trap! I want her to come after me! Let's see what she is made of,' cried MM with vengeance and anger as he spoke. Even MM was living for days like these!

Rathod's heart skipped a few beats at the very thought of another bloody face-off. He was already sweating profusely as he turned towards the glass cage. He was startled to see the python quietly gobbling down an entire rabbit in one go.

CHAPTER 7

Yesterdays and Tomorrows

Present day
MM's residence, Powai

It was an extremely cloudy morning in Mumbai and the rain was just about setting itself up for a grand entry. Ricky was doing his routine laps in the swimming pool and Billu was working out with weights just by the pool. Pravi was watching the news on TV, sitting in the living room, catching glimpses of Ricky swimming in the pool. The house was pretty silent and everyone was quietly going about their business except for the news reader on TV, whose voice alone was loud and clear. In fact, loud enough to have woken up the red headed python, who was otherwise in a lazy, sleepy mood.

'Top Bollywood actress Zara found dead in her bedroom under mysterious circumstances! Breaking news! Breaking news! Breaking news!' the anchor announced three times in a shrill voice, before moving onto the details.

There was a huge splash in the pool as MM rocketed out from under water. 'Arey baba! What a beautiful woman she was! How good all her item numbers were! Even yesterday I was watching her songs in the bathroom. What a sad end and what a great loss to this nation,' mourned MM after he jetted out from beneath. He was supposedly doing underwater yoga, which he had once seen on an English television show.

'Oye Ricky! You are not Zara's fan?' he asked.

'I'm everybody's fan, bhai. I like all kinds of actresses and women,' Ricky replied.

'You naughty boy!' MM gave Ricky a wily smile.

Pravi had walked out to the pool by now.

'Vivank and his friend are starting their scout work from tomorrow it seems,' she told Ricky.

'Yeah! Vivank has informed me as well. He's good. I'm sure he will pick up some really exciting talent,' Ricky replied.

'Let's see. Anyway, you support him too much. I know you are a big fan of his game and all that, but I still feel it's a huge risk,' Pravi retorted.

'Which is why I have tagged his friend with him, to keep a watch on him and keep him under control,' Ricky replied.

'What are you two talking about?' MM interjected.

'Our team coach and his friend, bhai,' Ricky replied.

'Are they trustworthy?' MM asked suspiciously, as always.

'They won't cause us any trouble. The coach had a troublesome past. He used to be a powder addict but he is now clean,' answered Ricky.

'Hahahaha! Like owner, like MD, like COO, like coach! We should have named our team—the Powai Powders,' MM added rather proudly.

'Then matches would have been played in jail,' laughed Billu, lifting weights.

'How is the team shaping up otherwise?' MM asked Pravi.

'Player auction is next month. Before that we need to finalise our four outstation players and submit to the board. Hope those two pick up some useful players,' said Pravi in a doubtful tone.

One of Billu's men walked up to MM with a sheet of paper.

'What is it?' asked MM disdainfully.

'A note from the colonel, bhai,' the guy replied.

MM's body language changed as soon as he heard the word 'colonel'. He frantically splashed across the water and got out of the pool. He quickly crossed over to where the man stood and snatched the letter and opened it.

His hands were trembling and his heart was beating fast as he started reading the note.

But as MM finished reading, his eyes started glowing.

'Expected news. Nothing to worry. Tomorrow night it is guys. Be ready. Near the rock cliff by the port,' said MM to his team, in a subtle yet fiery tone.

'Who is this colonel, bhai? A big player?' asked Ricky immediately.

'He is big, Ricky. Bigger than players like us. I'll explain everything to you when the time comes,' replied MM.

'Come on, bhai! Who can be bigger in this game than us? You are the king of this jungle,' exclaimed Ricky.

'Arey Ricky, If I'm the king then he is the god of this jungle! Anyways let's focus on tomorrow. I decided to conduct this operation at this critical period precisely to cull out that pig Zia. Cull out the pig, so that we can then begin our operations smoothly,' said MM.

'Your end is tomorrow, Zia. Let me see how you escape from my clutches tomorrow,' hissed MM before going back under water with a new-found confidence.

Terminal 1, Mumbai Airport

Vivank and Cheeku sat in the food court as they waited to board their flight to Srinagar.

'Have you given up on Leepa?' asked Cheeku.

'Why do you say so?' asked Vinank.

'Because I felt so. All you do is stalk her on Facebook and Twitter. Otherwise there has been absolutely no serious effort from your side, apart from a foolish idea like this!' replied Cheeku.

'Foolish idea? Like what?' asked Vinank.

'Like going to Kashmir for scouting now, just because Leepa is from Kashmir!' answered Cheeku.

'This is not a foolish idea and I haven't given up on her,' Vivank reiterated strongly.

'Maybe she has given up on you and you don't want to accept that,' Cheeku tried to explain further.

That was one among the zillion occasions when Vivank felt like thrashing Cheeku. It was just because of the faith, trust and friendship between them that Vivank spared Cheeku every single time, despite his annoying attitude.

Though he was angry with Cheeku, Vivank too, was starting to fear that Leepa may not return to his life again.

'You really think she has moved on?' he asked Cheeku like a child.

'Aur kya? We tried contacting her office as soon you finished your rehab. They said she had wilfully gotten herself transferred to Delhi. We even tried to track her in Delhi but no one could give us a proper response. Agreed, the tracking was not fool proof, but what about her? She meticulously completed the "post-breakup procedure" of relocating, changing her phone number, changing her email address and blocking you on social media! She has chucked

you out of her real and virtual life. How could someone be more specific than this in trying to convey something? Please tell.' asked Cheeku.

'Err…but…for four years she was following me sincerely. What do you have to say to that?' Vivank was fast losing hope, yet somehow, wanted to hear some hopeful things from Cheeku.

'Those four years were before she met you. Then she didn't know the real you! Once she met you, she got to know the real you and the rest is history!' Cheeku was laughing as he spoke but felt really sad for Vivank.

Vivank knew it was only a joke, but today, he didn't have Leepa by his side and that was all that mattered.

'Yeah! Nobody likes me,' Vivank said in a sad tone.

'Now don't feel sad. Forget all that. Surely, she would have come back to you had she really wanted to. So, leave all that. You have so much to look forward to. A fantastic prospect of coaching a cricket team to glory in a T20 league. Whatever you couldn't achieve as a player I'm sure you'll achieve as a coach. Don't let anyone or anything come between you and this opportunity!' replied Cheeku.

'I accept all that but I'm not giving up on her yet!' Vivank spoke with sad yet steely resolve.

Two thoughts occupied Vivank's divided heart and mind—one was a sense of excitement for being back in the world of cricket and the other a sense of loss for not having Leepa by his side. Vivank had restarted his fitness routine and was slowly getting back to his competitive fitness level. As much as cricket was propelling Vivank forward, Leepa's thoughts were pulling him back. Her thoughts were pulling him back to an abyss from which he feared he would never escape. As much as Vivank didn't want to fall into that abyss, everything around him reminded him of her.

Two years ago
Terminal 1, Mumbai Airport

'Sugarcane juice?! How can anyone drink such gross amounts of sugarcane juice?' Vivank laughed when Leepa brought a huge pitcher of sugarcane juice, as they were waiting to board the plane from Mumbai airport for one of Vivank's away matches.

'Sugarcane juice is healthy!' Leepa advocated.

'Yeah yeah! Please drink to your heart's content,' Vivank trolled her.

Leepa suddenly got up and frantically ran to hide behind Vivank and turned to the other side.

'My boss! My boss! Oh my god! I'm finished today! I'm not supposed to be here!' she was frantically whispering to Vivank.

'So what? Why do you bother? I thought you were on leave?' Vivank asked curiously.

'Yeah? You think it's your *baap ka bank*? Who will give me leave every week to follow you to all your cricket matches?' Leepa was turning away and talking in a jittery and tensed tone.

'I feel like I am in school again!' she said as she walked further away to a chair and sat in the corner facing the glass wall, which led onto the parking bays of the planes. She pulled out her charger and plugged in her phone, pretending to charge her phone.

Bending towards the phone that was still connected to the charging point, she called Vivank.

'I was supposed to be attending my grandmother's aunt's funeral!' Leepa whispered into the phone.

'This is hilarious. I'm unable to control my laughter. Does your grandmother really have an aunt?' asked Vivank.

'No! In a similar vein, I've so far killed three of my relatives, admitted seven of them to the hospital after a car crash, and I was also rejected by three bridegrooms who came to see me in the past four months. This and more only to be with you every time!' replied an irritated Leepa.

Vivank really felt touched. He had never experienced true love before and resolved to never let her go. But all this was when he was sober.

Present day
Terminal 1, Mumbai Airport

Vivank was staring sadly at the sugarcane juice shop which was right in front of him at the airport. A couple was cuddling, laughing and buying themselves cane juice.

'Come, boarding has started. First assignment of your second innings. Let's go,' Cheeku called out.

∞

Zia's residence, Bandra

'One company of 12 on the southern end and one more company of 12 on the north-western end. My vehicle will stop near the customs check-post. Rathod and I will walk in with 10 other men up to rock cliff, Himanshu would stay back and guide the companies outside,' Zia was busy making her plans for the next day.

The news of MM's meeting with international drug dealers the next day had reached her and she was busy setting up a meticulous plan to nab MM. Zia was standing on the terrace in her pyjamas with Rathod and Himanshu.

Tracking and hunting them down was the only thing that was running through her mind. From the moment she had gotten the information, she couldn't think about anything else, other than planning this operation.

'Track their phones and keep me updated about their movements. We need to wait until all of them arrive,' she was letting her instructions flow.

'About nine people are expected to meet MM and his gang, ma'am. We still have no information on the kind or quantity of goods,' Rathod said.

'What's the source?' Zia still wasn't sure.

'A local dealer called Rodriguez, ma'am. He does some petty supply here and there. Whoever pays him is his boss,' Rathod replied.

'Hmm...let's see. Even if it's just eight or nine of them, let's not underestimate things,' Zia made it clear.

'Ma'am, it's a big and a risky operation for sure. We are still not sure about the goods. Are we putting ourselves in a dangerous situation?' Himanshu asked.

'As police personnel, we are in a dangerous situation every single day anyway, even without realising. Doing it tomorrow or not at all isn't even a question. How to go about the operation is what I've been thinking about all day, before deciding on the formation that I just briefed you with,' the cool cop was speaking in her usual fearless tone.

Seeing the target in proximity with all the ammunition in her hand was a sight that every honest police officer waits for, and Zia's wait was about to be over. Her frustration had completely vanished and her focus now, was her target. The big, fat, round target, waiting to be brutally attacked!

'Open fire only on my instructions. Don't use the common wireless channel. Use the second channel that Himanshu has given us. That's it from me. See you all tomorrow at the game,' Zia spoke with utmost confidence and walked down the stairs.

'What a classy night it's going to be,' MM gave the wildest possible roar as he overheard everything through Rathod's phone, which was connected to MM's own phone and discreetly placed in his pockets!

'After tomorrow night, only one of us will live to see the sunrise! No prizes for guessing who!' MM was at his arrogant best as he was getting ready to have a shot at his enemy again.

MM and Ricky were drinking away ahead of what could be, the bloodiest night they had ever seen in their lives!

CHAPTER 8

Balls and Bullets

'Surgical strike! That's exactly where the surgical strikes by our army took place recently!' said a proud cab driver when Cheeku asked him about Leepa Valley.

Vivank and Cheeku had just landed in Srinagar to scout outstation players for their MSL team. It was spring and all of Kashmir, with its apples, cherries, pears, tulips, peaches and almonds, was at its cheerful best! Freshness and fragrances were oozing all over the place, as every part of the city looked soaked in the beauty of spring.

Vivank and Cheeku were looking out of their windows as the cab drove into the city.

'Leepa Valley, Kel and Battal were the main places targetted. About 80 Pakistani militants were killed,' added the driver.

'Is there a way we can reach Leepa Valley?' Vivank had been waiting to ask this question ever since he had landed in Kashmir.

'Hahahaha! Have you really come to select players for your cricket team or are you some secret agents that they show in the movies?' the cab driver asked laughingly.

Vivank had come to Kashmir only to lose himself in Leepa's memories. Having followed all the political and military situations between India and Pakistan on television, Vivank knew that his chances of visiting Leepa Valley were bleak but was still desperately hoping for some miracle to happen.

'So, no chance?' he asked the cab driver again.

'No chance, boss! Earlier, the Muzaffarabad bus services used to issue travel permits to Srinagar. Karavan-e-aman weekly bus services used to operate from Srinagar to Muzaffarbad, covering about 170 kilometres through rough terrains, crossing the LoC.

Even that would have taken you only up to Muzaffarbad. From there you had to travel another 100 kilometres into "Azad Kashmir" to reach Leepa Valley. But you can't go there now. All operations have been shut since the surgical strike last month,' the driver clarified.

'When do you think the services will resume?' Vivank was as desperate as a kid looking for his lost toy.

'Hopefully, soon. You follow our PM's Twitter handle. You will get instant information on all these things,' said the cab driver as he dropped them at the hotel.

'I've spoken to the cricket association secretary here. He was very helpful. He has asked some promising under-19 boys to come for net practice tomorrow morning. See you at 7 a.m. Goodnight,' Cheeku was visibly pleased, having done his homework meticulously, as he stepped into his room bidding goodnight to Vivank.

'Goodnight,' replied a tired Vivank, as he entered his room.

He was more mentally tired than physically. He still had no clue about Leepa. When Cheeku was scouting locations, the first place that struck Vivank was Kashmir. Leepa would so often speak of the beauty of Kashmir! Vivank and Leepa had in fact been planning to visit Kashmir the week after Goa. And then the Goa debacle happened. Now, he was in Kashmir, but she wasn't with him.

Two years ago
Mumbai

'That's my favourite—chicken yakhni pulao. This is rogan josh, which I'm sure you would have eaten in many North Indian restaurants, but this one is authentic. This is matschgand made from minced meatballs. This is yoghurt lamb curry. So yummy. Isn't it?' Leepa explained the dishes to Vivank as they scanned the buffet at the Kashmiri food festival in Mumbai. The name of every dish was neatly written with a detailed description beneath the vessels on the buffet table, but Vivank pretended not to have seen them so he could listen to Leepa's commentary!

'This is haak, Kashmiri equivalent of spinach. I don't like it. You won't like it either!' She actually went to the length of discarding the haak portions from Vivank's plate.

Vivank absolutely loved everything about her. Her unflinching love for him, unbelievable levels of affection and even her obsessive intrusion into everything Vivank did.

'Don't ever lie to me about anything in your life. Important or trivial, I need to know everything. Please don't ever hide anything from me,' she would keep telling Vivank.

'What would you do if I hid something?' Vivank would chuckle and ask just for fun's sake.

'I would surely leave you.' Each time her answer would be the same. Vivank had never imagined that she would actually leave him one day!

Present day
Kashmir

'How can someone be angry for so long?'
 'What if she is also in Kashmir now?'
 'Has she gone back to her ancestral place?'
 'What if something happened to her during the surgical strikes?'
 'Or has she moved on?'
 'Is she in another relationship now?'

Exhausted with thousand such questions crossing his mind, Vivank fell asleep.

∞

Sher-i-Kashmir Cricket Ground, Srinagar

Spine-chilling cold winds blew across the lush green grass of the cricket ground, dew drops on the grass making the ground look like a pearl carpet. Birch, deodar and willow trees surrounded the picturesque ground situated in the heart of Srinagar. A group of boys were seen warming up near the nets silently. The only sound other than the winds were the birds chirping all around the ground.

Vivank and Cheeku walked towards the centre-wicket where a tall man in cricketing gear stood smoking—breathing out poison into an otherwise pristine environment.

'Good morning, Kamran ji', wished Cheeku.

'Good morning, saab!' He wished back.

'Kamran ji, this is Vivank,' introduced Cheeku.

'I know, I know, saab! He is a hero in the domestic circuit,' Kamran said as he offered a cigarette to Vivank.

Vivank extended his hand involuntarily and looked at the Cheeku.

Only after seeing the kind of look that Cheeku gave Vivank, did he realise what he was doing and immediately pulled away from the act.

'Thankfully!' murmured Cheeku.

'These boys are very good. They are all part of the J&K under-19 team. Do have a look,' Kamran invited them to the nets.

Vivank had a close look at each and every player on display in the nets, while Cheeku recorded the performance of a some of the boys. Vivank then padded up and faced a few bowlers.

They sweated it out for the next two hours, as the sun started making a slow, yet a grand entry.

Vivank and Cheeku then thanked the boys, wished them luck, and ended the practice session. 'Thank you, Kamran ji, we will discuss with team management and let you know.' They bid farewell and started walking out.

'The boys are very good but somehow the X factor is missing! I want to get an exceptional fast bowler for the team. These kids are good but no one is exceptional. We could get similar talent in Mumbai circles. I want an out-and-out fast-bowler, someone who can surprise everyone.' Vivank was speaking with a lot of passion after a long time.

'Sir, please have a look at my son Irfan,' Malik, the gatekeeper of the ground said.

'I heard Kamran saab talking to the kids about you coming today. My son Irfan is an exceptional fast-bowler, saab. Unfortunately, he is unable to play regularly as he must work in the fields to support our big family. Only we both work to support our large family of 12 members, Malik continued, hopeful for a positive response.

'Okay! Ask him to come in the afternoon,' Vivank replied

immediately as through life experiences, he had himself understood the value of an opportunity.

∞

'Oh my god!' exclaimed Cheeku in disbelief as Vivank was clean bowled by Irfan three times in a row.

Irfan was a 6-foot-4-inches tall, lanky, 16-year-old kid who was breathing fire with each delivery. He had height and brute power with which he propelled the ball to ridiculous speeds.

His long hair swung all over his face, making it even more difficult for the batsmen facing him.

'I think you should use a head band to tie your hair, Irfan. It will help you focus better. It's as much a distraction for you as it is for the batsman,' Vivank later advised him.

Irfan, though a shy and a soft-spoken boy, was chuffed, hearing the encouraging words from Vivank and Cheeku.

Malik couldn't contain his happiness. He requested Vivank to give his son an opportunity.

Vivank too was super excited to see Irfan perform. 'This boy is a special talent. We don't have a speedometer here but I'm sure he bowls at 150 kmph and above with substantial swing. He looks very fit too. He just needs to improve his armoury and develop other facets like the slower ball, cutters, etc. to help him and to survive conditions that may not be conducive to his style of bowling,' he told Malik, as Cheeku and Irfan listened keenly.

'See you in Mumbai soon,' Vivank waved at Irfan, as Cheeku and him got into their cab.

'I know you took this journey because you wanted to see Leepa's place, but it has turned out to be a master stroke. I don't think other teams will scout so deep. Kudos!' Cheeku wished his coach officially!

'Moral of the story is that Leepa will always do me good, whether she is by my side or not. So, I suggest we go on a Leepa memory trail. I'm sure we'll get few more good players.' Vivank sounded casual, but he had played this sentence about a thousand times in his mind before uttering it.

'Nobody else in the history of the game has scouted for players this way! Using their ex-girlfriend's memory trails,' Cheeku said with a roaring laughter.

'Ex nahi baba, sirf girlfriend bolo,' Vivank corrected him with a smile.

∞

'Only one of us will live to see the sunrise tomorrow,' Zia quietly promised herself, as she was leaving her office to embark upon her quest to finish MM forever.

'Are you sure that they're meeting at the rock cliff?' she asked Rathod.

'Yes, ma'am. All our sources point to the rock cliff. Of late, a couple of Columbian nationals, reportedly smugglers, have been frequently talking to MM's men. We're tracking their movements and calls continuously, ma'am. They are moving towards the rock cliff as we speak, ma'am!' Rathod replied.

Zia's heart was pounding as she got into her jeep. Something was clearly not right and she could sense it.

For most of her life, she had overcome all the adversities that had come her way. She had single-handedly brushed aside all the life-threatening conditions that she encountered during the course of her career, but this one was tricky. MM was hurt and was looking for vengeance. She wasn't sure if she was fully prepared for this face-off. She knew that she was taking a huge risk. A risk that may even cost her own life. She was the cool cop on the outside, but deep inside her heart was fluttering.

Having encountered death from close quarters quite a few times, every survival made her fear death more. The very thought of not being there to see tomorrow haunted her immensely.

'I'll survive today! I'll survive today!' she nervously kept repeating to herself, as her jeep sped towards the rock cliff.

The rock cliff was the extreme edge of a huge hill that separated the sea and Dongri town. There were two entry points—the north way and the south way—both of which had bushy uphill pathways covered with dense vegetation for about a kilometre before one could reach the rock cliff. All of Zia's team, including Zia herself, were in plain clothes. Zia, Rathod and Himanshu were dressed in white shirts and khaki pants. They had all reached the entry spot as soon as they received information that all of MM's men and his international associates had reached the rock cliff.

They sent their hired taxis and jeeps to be stationed 1 kilometre away. One company of 12 armed policemen were stationed at the northwestern entrance, another company of 12 armed policemen were stationed at the south entrance. Himanshu was given the responsibility of controlling the entrance/exits points, as Zia and Rathod went all out with the attack. There were 44 of them, including Zia, which was roughly more than twice of what MM had inside.

Zia, Rathod and 20 other men took the south entrance and started moving towards the rock cliff. Suddenly, Zia stopped and instructed Rathod and a team of 10 to enter through the northern pathway.

'I'll not open fire. No one will open fire without my instruction, or unless they open fire at us. Rathod and team will wait near the view point that opens down into the rock cliff. I'll go this way and wait right behind the biggest peepal tree, near that rabbit mound. That's the point where one can have the clearest shot of the rock cliff.' Zia clearly spelt out her instructions and started moving briskly towards the rabbit mound.

Suddenly, there were serial gun shots that were heard from all directions. Zia was sure that the sound originated from the rock cliff. It was dark but the lights from the port nearby were enough to see who was who in the night. She saw one of her men getting injured from the shot. She had no time to think or be afraid in midst of the mayhem. She pulled out her pistol and started firing unscrupulously.

While everyone knew there were only two exit points, MM always had a third exit. He had the sea with him, as always. His men climbed down the ropes into a boat that was stationed beneath the rock cliff. MM had clearly outwitted Zia and was escaping through the sea. Calling her forces to seal the northwest and south exits, would be in vain as MM would have left by the time they reached. Zia continued to shoot, hoping to trace and nip out MM. A tall African man was shot on both his knees. But despite being shot, he was being pulled in by MM's men and dragged down, onto the boat.

Zia was desperately looking for MM but she couldn't find him.

MM was also looking for Zia and he found her, clearly standing behind the peepal tree waiting to have a shot at him. Ricky threw a Smith & Wesson 500 to MM, which MM caught and aimed at Zia. He shot—one, two, three bullets! Right on target!

'How classy these old-fashioned revolvers are,' he said with a vengeful smile, as he was the last one to be pulled down the rope and into the boat.

CHAPTER 9

Twists and Turns

The sound of police and ambulance sirens was deafening. In the wee hours of the morning, the rock cliff was teeming with police personnel conducting a thorough search operation.

About three police officers were injured and one police officer was killed in the line of duty.

Himanshu was walking breathlessly towards the peepal tree. The one with whom he worked so closely was now lying dead.

Himanshu was almost in a state of shock, as he saw the body lying beneath the tree. Brutally shot and torn open with bullets, there lay Inspector Rathod.

Lost his way. Lost his integrity. Lost his loyalty. And here he was lying motionless after losing his life. His dead eyes reflected his pain and spoke more truth now than they ever had done when Rathod was alive.

Zia meanwhile had just got into her vehicle and was on her way back home.

Police Headquarters, Crawford Market, Mumbai

It was late in the evening, roughly about 12 hours since the rock cliff shoot-out.

'Tiwary saab, Tiwary Saab!' 'Commissioner Sir!', called out the members of the press as Manish Tiwary entered office in a hurry.

As he heard the reporters calling out his name, he turned back and walked towards them.

'What happened at the rock cliff today, sir? Who killed Inspector Rathod? Was a smuggling racket being busted?'

Tiwary was bombarded with questions before he had even spoken a word.

Tiwary, the Mumbai city police commissioner, was quite an old hand at handling press meets. He knew when to talk, when not to talk, when to create drama, when to sound heroic and when to sound comical. 25 years in police service had made him 'seasoned' and 'accustomed'.

'We're looking into it! We will let you know once we make headway. We have to look into all the aspects. At this juncture, neither can we rule out anything, nor can we confirm anything. We're at it,' he repeated these sentences for the barrage of questions thrown at him.

Tiwary walked away at the same speed that he had walked in. He didn't talk to anybody on the way. He called for Zia as soon as he entered his chamber.

Zia walked in and sat casually, as if nothing had happened.

'Who the hell do you think you are?' The entire office would have heard Tiwary's voice, if not for the well-constructed acoustics in his room.

'Sir?' Zia gave a cool-cop-type reply.

'Stop your drama right there!' He signalled a harsh warning, pointing fingers at her in the most disdainful way.

'You've made a fool of yourself and the department with this operation,' he continued harshly.

'Sir, I'm not a fool and I don't intend to make a fool out of anybody, let alone the department!' Zia replied. She was trying hard to be calm but Tiwary was chipping away at her composure with every word.

'Shut up! Just shut up!' Tiwary was on her even before she could think of her next line.

'Cool. Cool. No words. All the hard work would be a waste,' she kept egging herself on to keep calm.

'Who authorised you to undertake this operation? Who authorised you to draw personnel from other wings? Who authorised you to tap phones and pump a major part of our intelligence resources into this?' The questions kept coming one after the other.

Zia kept quiet.

'Tell me! Will you answer the press outside?' Tiwary literally shouted at her face.

'Sir, I honestly suspected a huge drug racket. Which is why I had to use the kind of resources and energy that I did,' Zia replied.

'All right. You'll never learn. Did you have any concrete evidence about smuggling activities at the place you carried out the operation? And the area doesn't even fall under your jurisdiction, for your kindest information!'

'I agree, sir!'

'Did you get hold of any material evidence or proof about smuggling activities at the spot of your operation during or after your supposed operation?' asked Tiwary.

'No, sir,' Zia replied.

'I'll have to initiate a department-level enquiry against you for this. And one more wrong move or unnecessary activity from your side, you'll face the consequences!' Tiwary sternly looked deep into her eyes and uttered the last words.

Zia got up slowly, turned around and walked away.

Her face broke into a gentle smile as she walked towards the door. She slowly opened the door and quietly closed it behind her.

∽

It was around midnight. Zia was standing on the terrace of her apartment alone with a cup of green tea. She was peacefully sipping her cup of tea, looking at the ever-bustling city and appreciating its charm.

A message tone beeped suddenly. It was from Himanshu. The message read,

> 'Ma'am, I'm waiting outside and I request permission to talk to you for a few minutes.'

Zia asked him to come up and he was there two minutes later.

'You look so happy, ma'am. Very calm, relaxed and peaceful,' Himanshu started.

Zia smiled and prepared a long 'cool cop' answer but Himanshu interrupted her and said 'You look so happy that anyone who saw you now would think that today's operation was actually a success, ma'am.'

'What?' Zia gave him a surprised look.

'That route change and then calling Rathod to the peepal tree alone. Only you, Rathod and I were on that frequency ma'am,' Himanshu said with a smile.

'So what?' Zia had a surprised look on her face.

'So nothing, ma'am, Rathod was a very wrong man. I was initially shocked but reasoned out everything later,' Himanshu said.

'Go ahead, tell me what you have reasoned out, detective Himanshu?' a smiling Zia asked.

'You repeatedly spelt out your position, as you wanted Rathod to hear it and convey the location to MM. Once you and Rathod were alone together you beat him up black and blue until he was unconscious. You then tied him to the peepal tree and put an unloaded gun in his hands so that MM would think it was you who was trying to gun him down from behind the peepal tree.' Zia clapped softly as she heard Himanshu.

'Also, you intentionally planned that all three of us wear similar attires. Brilliant, ma'am!' Himanshu said in a proud tone.

Zia wore a happy smile.

'Rathod was disloyal, corrupt and on MM's side. You knew all this beforehand. Knowing this, you planned the operation with Rathod in the core team? Why ma'am?' Himanshu asked.

'Think, you'll have the answer,' said Zia sipping her tea.

'You knew you needed more evidence to destroy MM. You also couldn't sit idle and put us in a weaker position. Hence, you planned this operation not to destroy MM but to destroy Rathod! Masterstroke, ma'am! But I still have a doubt, ma'am?' continued Himanshu.

'Go ahead!' replied Zia.

'Going by your setup, I'm sure you had a clear shot at MM, ma'am. Why didn't you take it and finish it once for all?' asked Himanshu.

'Because then things wouldn't end once and for all, Himanshu ji! There are larger games at play here,' replied a confident Zia.

'Oh! I'm sure you have all the plans ready, ma'am. I'll always be ready for your orders for this mission, ma'am!'

Himanshu had lot of respect for Zia, which was evident from his tone and body language.

'Well. There are good things and there are bad things, then there are Zia things, Himanshu ji. Glad that you understood them. Have some tea before you leave,' replied Zia.

Zia had set Rathod up, succeeded in her objective, outwitted MM into a false shoot-out and made MM run away right in front of her eyes. She was now plotting her next moves to destroy MM, as she walked quietly to the kitchen with a broad smile on her face to bring some tea for Himanshu.

Just as Himanshu was about to leave, Zia said softly 'Himanshu ji, just enquire casually among our sources in the drug market for a man called "the colonel".'

'The colonel? Ma'am? In the drug market?'

'Yes,' confirmed Zia.

∞

'I've been to this place before with Leepa,' Vivank pointed at Bara Imambara, as he and Cheeku drove past it on a sunny morning in crowded Lucknow.

From Srinagar they had reached Lucknow the previous night and were on their way to scout their next outstation player.

'Yes, I remember you coming here with her for your zonal five-day game,' Cheeku replied.

'Yeah. It was raining heavily that day. We were treating ourselves to tunday kebabs in our room when Leepa suddenly had a craving for rose falooda!' Vivank recollected.

'Oh yes! Rose falooda is quite famous here! Wish we could

have it too today! Were you able to get it for her that day?' asked an inquisitive Cheeku.

'Yes, but after a lot of effort. It was raining heavily and there was a massive traffic jam. After waiting in vain for a taxi, I finally took a lift to the rose falooda shop in old Lucknow, borrowed an umbrella from that gentleman who gave me the lift, and went to buy some falooda. Took double lifts in two wheelers and got back to the hotel,' Vivank remembered smilingly.

'Wow! That's amazing! Any woman would have loved it,' Cheeku said.

'Yeah, she loved it. Until…' Vivank spoke hesitantly.

'Until what?' Cheeku asked sounding confused.

'Until she realised that I also got powder on the way back,' Vivank replied slowly.

'This's exactly why she left you and why everyone gave up on you. Just when we pin our hopes on you, you fail us!' Cheeku said in a disappointed tone.

Vivank didn't reply. He silently put his head down.

Not wanting to hurt Vivank anymore, Cheeku changed the topic.

'I hope we have some time after the selection trials. I want to take some more photos for my Instagram!' Cheeku proudly said.

Vivank, as Cheeku expected, lifted his head up and resumed conversing.

'What about the pictures that you took in Kashmir? You made me stand in freezing cold to click your pictures with all the filters and depth effects. But you haven't uploaded even a single pic yet?' Vivank asked in a sad yet curious tone.

'Hold on, brother. I'll go home and start releasing my pictures one-by-one. #ThrowbackThursday, #FlashbackFriday,

#SundayFunday—so many hashtags are there. Wait and watch my fireworks!'

Cheeku boasted.

Soon they were at the YMCA cricket ground. Cheeku couldn't properly connect with the state association heads, so they tried to look at the resources available on hand.

A group of boys were playing a practice match, Vivank and Cheeku sat in the gallery with binoculars and watched the game.

'You should have confirmed with the coordinators before starting. We are foolishly sitting and watching kids play a match,' Vivank almost scolded Cheeku.

'I know I, should have tied up things and then brought you here, but we are running out of time. The player auction is only three weeks away and we need to make a lot of preparations for it. Plus, your highness strictly mentioned that you wanted to travel through your "Leepa love route"! That left us with limited options and uncooperative associations,' Cheeku tried to justify.

'Hmmm!' Vivank didn't really try to reason with Cheeku, he was already absorbed in the 'kiddy' match.

'Look at that kid. Fourth wicket already for him. And he has bowled only two overs,' Vivank sounded truly excited.

'Who, that left arm spinner?' Cheeku asked.

'Yeah, he is mixing up Chinaman and orthodox left arm spin. Looks wily,' Vivank said.

'Wily here. Yes. But there they will sort him in a few balls. Everyone has video recording and analysing facilities these days!' Cheeku replied, still unconvinced.

'We're anyway planning to get a frontline spinner at the auction, why don't we get this kid and drop a surprise?' Vivank sounded fully convinced.

'Your call, coach!' replied Cheeku.

The kid picked up a couple more wickets in quick succession and the opposition collapsed like a stack of cards.

'Rajawat, sir. Saurav Kumar Rajawat,' the boy replied. He had just turned 16, and had apparently made heads turn in his age group's cricket circuit.

'I'm ready to come any time, sir. I want to be the best bowler in the world. I want to win,' he said confidently and spontaneously.

Cheeku spoke to Rajawat's parents and coach, and completed all the formalities to get him to Mumbai for MSL.

With Rajawat, the Dragons had just signed their second player. They had two outstation bowlers now. Both 16 years of age, with contrasting capabilities—one out-and-out fast bowler and the other a foxy left arm spinner.

'Investing heavily in inexperienced youth. Let's see,' said Cheeku as he started loading their data on his laptop.

'These boys will give their everything and play with hunger and fire to succeed. That hunger and fire is important. It is that kind of team that I wish to build. I'm sure that these boys will make us proud.' said Vivank as they finished their day's work and went around Lucknow to complete Cheeku's photo session.

CHAPTER 10

Threads and Notes

'Oh! Is it? Can you please tell me which branch she is posted at currently?' Vivank was on call with an executive from Imperial Bank.

'Any luck?' asked Cheeku, as he was packing his bag for their next visit.

'Not much.' Vivank gave the usual negative reply that he had been hearing for months now, and then suddenly realised that he might have a breakthrough.

'Well maybe, yes'! he continued, 'I checked with one of their offices in Delhi. Sonu's wife has just joined that bank. She says that from the available records it seems that Leepa had first joined the Chanakyapuri branch when she came to Delhi. She doesn't have subsequent data or at least is unable to access other data for now.' He was beginning to feel happy.

But his mood dipped as he uttered the next sentence.

'Uncertainty and ignorance could still be better than another insult or heartbreak,' he said.

He was unsure about pursuing Leepa.

By the time Vivank had gone through his spectrum of emotions, Cheeku was on another call.

'No one cares about my emotions,' Vivank sighed as he realised Cheeku wasn't around when he finished.

'How's it going?' It was Ricky's voice on the other end. Pravi too was on the line as it was a conference call.

'Good. We have two kids. They are very good. Irfan is an exceptional fast bowler and the other kid, Rajawat, is a left arm mystery spinner,' replied Cheeku.

'Cool. How many more do you intend to pick?' Ricky asked.

'One more maybe. Rules allow for four outstation players in the squad, but only two can play in the team. We don't want two players wasting their potential on the bench. Also, Vivank is making a list of potential targets for us at the auction with specific skill sets. We can have a meeting once we finalize the third player. I have mailed the same to Pravi this morning,' Cheeku explained their team building strategy.

'Ya! Got your mail, just wanted to confirm things,' Pravi chipped in.

'Okay. He's good otherwise? No old habits?' she asked cautiously.

'No, no! He has come miles away from that. I will let you know if anything of that sort happens,' Cheeku assured them and hung up.

It was 1 March on the calender and was Vivank's birthday month. His birthday was fast approaching and Vivank sat in his balcony thinking about the birthdays he had spent with Leepa.

They had made each other's birthdays extremely special, but Vivank was always touched by the extra mile that Leepa went and that extra bit of care she always put in.

Two years ago

'I want to celebrate your birthday, your life and everything about you! This book that I'm gifting you is just one of the ways to let you know just how special you are. Now make a wish!' she said and lit the candle on the cake for Vivank to blow out!

It was a beautiful customized cake in Vivank's favourite pineapple flavour. It depicted a cricket ground complete with a match and spectators and even a tiny fondant Vivank hitting the ball to the gallery!

Leepa urged Vivank to cut the cake as quickly as possible to childishly deny Cheeku his Instagram opportunity. With his parents joining in on a video call as well, that was one of his most memorable birthdays, Vivank thought.

It was his thirty-fifth birthday and Leepa, in addition to her handwritten book, had also given him 35 roses, lit 35 candles and had arranged a feast of 35 food items from around the world that Vivank loved! She had also given him a goody bag of 12 small personalized gifts, one for each month of the year. Though not very expensive, these objects were very dear to Vivank, reminding him that Leepa was still with him. And the book! It contained 365 wonderful things Leepa had to tell Vivank, one for each day of the year, written in the nicest possible way.

'This book is not enough to tell you how much I love you!' she would proudly say.

Present day

Vivank was now sitting with the same book in his balcony—that same balcony in front of which Leepa used to stop every day just to catch a glimpse of him.

He kept staring at the place where she used to stand. He found nothing but emptiness. On the outside and inside.

⁂

'Damn it! That rogue woman made me kill my own man!' MM was punching against the toughened glass wall of the python's cage as he burst out in anger. He punched with so much vigour that his lazy python turned its head up and gave him a prolonged stare.

'Send our men to her place. Let's finish her off tonight itself,' MM sounded angry and revengeful.

'Let's first finish our job, bhai. Hasty moves could deter our plans. Let's just get on with our work quickly. Also, Ricky has spoken to Tiwary saab to rein her in. She won't be carrying out her big operations anytime soon,' Billu tried to pacify MM.

MM looked at Ricky.

'Yes, bhai. Let's wait. Besides the cricket season is about to begin. We'll have to ignore her for now,' Ricky said.

'I'm not convinced. I will anyway discuss with the colonel and then take a call,' MM said, still in anger.

The doorbell rang.

'See! Doorbells and God approve of me,' MM exclaimed. Ricky and Billu looked at each other, not knowing if it was a joke or if he had meant it seriously.

The same man who had handed MM a note when they were by the pool came in with another note.

MM read it. 'Damn it!' He cried out angrily again. 'Let's hold off on Zia. But let our other operations continue as planned,' MM ordered.

Both Billu and Ricky nodded.

'How's Femi now? Poor guy from Africa…took such a nasty shot,' MM asked in a sorry childlike tone.

'Better now, bhai. We took him out of the hospital as soon as he was out of danger. We weren't sure if he would be safe there,' Billu said.

'Of course, it's unsafe for him to be at the hospital. Hope you didn't leave anything behind?' MM asked.

'No, bhai. We were extra careful with everything,' Billu replied.

'Be careful with this hospital situation. I'm sure that's the first place Zia will start digging. I don't want anything untoward to happen before the launch!' MM warned.

'Yes, bhai. Which is why we had admitted him to a hospital which was farthest away from the rock cliff, even if it meant losing out on valuable time immediately after his injury,' Billu replied.

'When is our "launch", bhai?' Billu asked in a soft tone.

'At the after-auction party in the hotel!' MM finally let out his trademark evil laugh.

∽

'We already have a list of city hospitals in our data base. Send teams to each of these hospitals and look for a tall and bald-headed African man in his early 40s,' Zia instructed.

'Will do, ma'am, but cannot do it all in one go. Tiwary saab has clearly instructed not to deploy or mobilise men for any operation without his concurrence, ma'am. We need to work with limited resources and with a trusted few men who are available,' Himanshu said.

'Start with the hospital farthest away from the cliff. I'm sure MM would guess that we would start with hospitals nearest to the rock cliff. And he would have admitted that African guy to the farthest possible place. Try looking for new admissions in the hospitals with the available details,' Zia said.

'Sure, ma'am,' replied Himanshu.

'Have you got the details about the consignment from China?' asked Zia.

'Yes, ma'am. I have an update on the consignment. Was about to inform you, ma'am.' replied Himanshu.

'Great. Has it reached?' asked Zia

'Yes, ma'am. The consignment from China was released from the port last week,' informed Himanshu.

'Oh! Where is it addressed to? Were you able to find that out?' Zia asked.

'RKM Residential School, Uttam Hill, ma'am. That is the school MM has recently acquired along with the cricket team, ma'am,' informed Himanshu.

'Yeah! But why would he place such costly orders for the school from a Chinese construction firm?' Zia thought loudly.

'That school ground is also the ground where his team will play all their home matches. For all we know, he really wants to improve the ground before the matches,' replied Himanshu.

'Biggest joke! You think he really cares about cricket or the school?' Zia laughed coupled with anger.

'We are going there tonight! To the school! Only the two of us. Let's try to find out what he is up to!' added Zia.

'Bhupinder Singh, the swashbuckling under-19 opening batsman from Punjab has agreed to sign with us as an outstation player,' Vivank told Cheeku as he shut down his laptop.

'How come?' Cheeku asked curiously.

'I spent quite some time with him at a school cricket camp, which I had inaugurated as a player. Just spoke to him on Skype.

He remembers everything I told him. Says he will be more than happy to play for the Dragons!' Vivank said calmly.

'Wow!' shouted Cheeku in jubilation.

But immediately stopped and remarked, 'Not wow! We should have gone to Punjab and done this, not on Skype. I missed my chance to Instagram from Punjab,' Cheeku said in a mixed tone.

'Why didn't you want to go? Is it not on the Leepa trails? I remember you guys travelling to Mohali once?' Cheeku continued.

'Yes, we had gone. I don't want to go again. It's becoming increasingly difficult and suffocating. Let's stop this Leepa thing and focus on cricket. We now have three players. Let's start marking up our players for the auction next week,' Vivank said.

His focus was as much on Leepa as it was on cricket, though he didn't want to admit it and wanted Cheeku to believe that he had finally moved on.

On the inside Vivank was crying and longing for Leepa. He was truly and madly in love with her. The fear of seeing her in another relationship was weighing heavy on him. He would often feel that his heart and mind were crushing under this weight.

There was only one thing that kept him going and it was cricket. The auction was soon approaching and he needed to focus!

'I have crucial information to share, ma'am. You were right! MM has been referring to some "colonel" when he talks about his business or makes decisions. Our earlier call recordings also confirm the same. Seems to me that this colonel is an important person in the whole scheme of things,' Himanshu informed Zia as they approached the RKM school compound.

'But no one has seen or met this colonel. It looks like he is right there yet he is not there! This colonel!' he continued.

'That's exactly what we need to do! Find this ghost called the colonel who seems to be controlling everything!' Zia said.

It was about 8 p.m. in the evening; they came in plain clothes and left their vehicles in a parking lot 2 kilometres away from the school compound and started walking with their press identity cards hung around their necks.

'Almost half the people in the city use these cards and stickers. Why not us,' laughed Himanshu referring to their identity cards.

'The other half uses our department cards and stickers,' chuckled Zia.

It was drizzling as they reached the school compound.

They helped each other climb over the wall into the school compound. Even at night there seemed to be quite a few people inside, and they could hear noises coming from behind the school building. Zia's heart started pounding. Himanshu didn't show any fear but he too, after seeing what had happened to Rathod, was extremely anxious.

'Have you loaded the gun?' she asked Himanshu.

'Yes, ma'am.'

'Don't fire unless you are told to,' Zia gave her orders.

They could hear their hearts pounding as they approached the point from where they could see what was happening on the other side of the school building. They looked across, holding their breath and guns.

About a hundred construction workers were working all over the cricket ground that was right behind the building and close to the hill. Almost 60–65 of them had gathered around to erect a pole, which looked to be part of the floodlights. Amidst the noise, one could spot the site-supervisor dishing out instructions to the workers.

'*Jaldi karo, jaldi karo,*' he was yelling at them repeatedly as he kept walking around the ground.

'What's happening?' Zia quietly asked a worker, posing as if they were press reporters.

'MSL matches start in a month. We are getting the ground ready,' he replied and walked away for a tea break.

'Oh! Is that all?' remarked a visibly confused Zia.

Slowly their anxiety levels came down, but Zia was visibly disappointed with the development.

'They are actually getting ready for the cricket tournament!' remarked Himanshu with a laugh.

Zia remained silent. Her brain was processing everything and looking for an answer.

They climbed off the wall again and walked towards their car.

Out of the blue, they heard a loud screeching noise.

It was a car that suddenly approached them at a very high speed without even sounding a horn.

It emerged from a blind spot and it was pretty much impossible for Zia or Himanshu to have seen it until it came within striking distance. All they could hear was the huge rattle that the car engine made.

With a huge thud, the car ran over them and sped past just as quickly as it had come out of the bushes.

MM looked out of the window from the front passenger seat with a gleam on his face.

'This time it's indeed her! I've seen it with my own eyes!' His voice was filled with cruel happiness.

'Yeah,' nodded Ricky as he drove their car to safety.

CHAPTER 11

Bid-ridden

Grand Season Hotel, Colaba

'You're sure Sameer will play this league?' Cheeku asked doubtfully again, unable to believe Vivank's proposal.

'I told you, I've spoken to him. He is not going to England. He will play the entire league. There is a huge possibility that other teams might think that Sameer won't be available for the entire league and teams may not bid very high for him,' Vivank said.

Sameer was the current India superstar and one of the top draws to endorse MSL. But as Vivank pointed out, it was unclear as to whether Sameer would play the entire MSL. Given Vivank's close acquaintance with him, having played along with him for many years in Mumbai colours, he had gotten direct confirmation about his availability for the tournament.

'Who all are the big-ticket picks?' Pravi asked.

Vivank, Cheeku, Ricky, Pravi and other support staff were sitting in a mini boardroom near the auction room where the auction was supposed to happen the next morning. Pravi was wondering if she could ask Ricky out that night after the discussion. She had such deep feelings for Ricky but couldn't convey it to him.

Most of the time they were surrounded by people, which made it impossible for her to share her private feelings with Ricky.

'Thankfully Billu isn't here,' she sighed, hoping for some alone time with Ricky post discussion.

Vivank in the meantime was spelling out his auction plans.

'The other top draws apart from Sameer are likely to be Tariq, the fast bowling all-rounder, Killi the left-handed opener, Shankar the swashbuckling Mumbai under-19 opener, Sohail the fast-bowling sensation, and Ritwik the left arm seamer. Among the spinners Ganesh and Ankit are likely to go big,' Vivank concluded.

'Solid middle order batsmen like Gautham, Mazumdar and Tony are also likely to go very high. I'm sure, we will find two openers who give us the much-required speedy start. After that it's the middle order that controls the game,' Cheeku added.

'Needless to say, all-rounders and death bowlers are gold in this format. Problem is we don't have class all-rounders other than Tariq, Kunal and Kulwinder in the auction pool. We surely need one of them,' Pravi chipped in.

Ricky was observing everything quietly. He asked Vivank for his sure shot list to pick at the auction.

Vivank gave the list to Ricky.

It read:

1. Sameer
2. Tariq
3. Killi
4. Tony
5. 1 out of Gautham/Mazumdar
6. 1 out of Ankit/Ganesh
7. 2 out of Prashant/Vivek/Sainath

8. 1 wicket keeper out of Navdeep/Akash/Vipin
9. 1 out of Neeraj/Ashish/Viraj
10. 1 out of under-19 seamers Trivedi/Salman/Pankaj
11. Wild card

'Plus, the three outstation picks Bhupinder, Irfan and Rajawat. This will roughly make our squad, if we manage to get the players we are eyeing,' Vivank told Ricky.

'Looks okay, but what about Kulwinder?' Ricky asked.

'He is in his own world most of the time; mostly zoned out as if some song is being played around him and butterflies flying around his head! He is talented but lacks focus and is extremely inconsistent,' Vivank explained.

'So, Tariq surely then?' Ricky asked.

'Think so. He's pretty good,' Vivank replied.

Their discussion continued well past midnight and it was only around 1 a.m. that they retired to their rooms.

'Happy Birthday!' Cheeku wished Vivank as he got into his room.

'Thanks Cheeku!'

'Didn't want to wish there and distract your focus. This is your year! You will show your worth to everyone. Goodnight!'

Vivank was truly excited about the auction. He had watched T20 league auctions on television and had been part of auctions as a player, but for the first time he was going to pick a team!

'This is going to be some experience,' he thought.

A sense of déjà vu was setting into Vivank.

Leepa! That feeling that she was with him was not leaving him.

Despite all the confusion and depressing logic against his love, he strongly felt that Leepa was still in love with him and had not moved on. He knew that he was hoping against hope, but at least there was that hope!

Vivank soon fell asleep, with excitement, eagerness and 'hope' in his heart.

∽

'We hardly get anytime to talk,' said Pravi.

Ricky and her were standing in the balcony of Ricky's room. Ricky just smiled.

'Ya. With all these people around,' he added.

'Ricky, I know you like me…' Pravi came straight to the point.

'Of course, I do like you dear,' Ricky replied.

'Like as in, not the "like" you think, it's like "like",' Pravi tried to explain.

'Yeah, I also like you, like the "like" you think only.'

'Who else do you like "like" that?'

'A lot…'

'Come on…stop playing with me….'

'I don't get it.'

'Means I like you. What does a girl mean when she says such things?'

'Oh! I get it now. Though generally girls mean the opposite of a lot of stuff they say and I'm pretty poor at interpreting them, but this I understand clearly,' replied Ricky.

'Understand what?' asked Pravi

'That you like me?!'

'So! What do you have to say to that?'

'Pravi dear, you know very well that we are all people who live on the edge…'

'So, that means it's a no!'

'No! It isn't like that…'

'Then what? And you said girls actually mean the opposite of a lot of stuff they say.'

Ricky laughed!

'Pravi, you know what? We both know that we are quite fond of each other. But I don't think this is the right time to talk about it. The auction is in the morning and then in the evening we have our launch. We both know how big it is! And how it could change all our fortunes. We still have a lot of time to figure out about ourselves. We will cross that bridge when we get to it…' Ricky replied.

'Fine,' Pravi answered and headed for her room. There was a lot of love even in that anger as she walked towards the door.

'You know what! When a girl says fine, it means "It's not fine and you are screwed",' she laughed.

Ricky smiled and waved her goodnight from the balcony.

∞

'Get ready quickly! It's getting late! The auction starts in half an hour,' Cheeku shouted from outside the door.

Vivank got out of his bed like an odd fish jumping out of a bowl and ran to the door.

Cheeku was dressed in a suit.

'What's this?' Vivank gave a sleepy laugh.

'This is how team management people dress-up for auctions!' Cheeku replied.

Vivank was still laughing.

'Okay fine,' Cheeku wasn't pleased.

'Show me your phone,' Vivank grabbed Cheeku's phone before he could say anything.

Vivank opened Instagram on Cheeku's phone. Cheeku had

already Instagrammed his picture with his suit on with the hashtags #MicDrop #NoMoreHashtags and then added about 10 more hashtags about the hotel and the player auction.

'You, had enough fun laughing at me! Now get ready. The auction starts in 15 minutes.'

'Shit man, I overslept and didn't realise it was time. Give me five minutes,' Vivank ran to the bathroom, changed his t-shirt and proudly wore the blue coloured Dongri Dragons jersey with practice shorts and came out.

'You must be the first person ever to enter a cricket player auction room dressed up like this,' it was Cheeku's turn to laugh.

They entered the auction room soon. The six competing teams were seated in round tables across the hall. The auctioneer Ramsay was busy setting up his auction table. Ricky and Pravi were already seated at the Dragons table.

'Ladies and gentlemen! Welcome to the inaugural MSL player auction. We have six teams today for the auction. Colaba Kings, Andheri Hawks, Dongri Dragons, Bandra Hurricanes, Powai Puff Boys and Juhu Titans. The inaugural MSL player auction has received a tremendous response and is already trending across all social media platforms. We have an enormous reach and I would like to thank the teams, sponsors and the players who have signed up for the league. Without further ado let's kick start the MSL player auction!' declared the Chairman of MSL.

'Happy Birthday, Vivank,' Ricky and Pravi wished him.

'Thank you!' Vivank thanked them without even looking at them. He was waiting for the auction to start like a kid waits for an avenger movie to start.

'When will they start. I can't wait for it to start,' he kept nagging Cheeku.

There was a beep on his phone.

'Happy Birthday, Vivank,' the text was from Leepa!

'Oh! My powder!' Vivank couldn't believe what he was seeing. It was from Leepa! His déjà vu had come true! This was incredible!

He immediately replied—'thanks, I love you' with hearts, kisses and every possible romantic emoji. But his reply didn't go through. He tried calling but the number was not reachable.

Sensing a distraction, Ricky gave Vivank a long, scornful look, which got him back to his senses. Vivank pulled out his auction notebook and got ready.

Within a minute, Vivank moved from one world to another world. There were only two people in that world. Him and Leepa.

Now he started nagging Cheeku, 'When will they end? I can't wait for them to end!'

'Hey! What's up with you! Are you fine? Or on powder? A couple of minutes earlier you said you couldn't wait for it to start. Now you say that you can't wait for it to end. What are you thinking?' Cheeku asked.

Vivank showed him Leepa's text. 'Oh my god. This can't be real!' a shocked Cheeku murmured.

'It is real you fool!' a restless Vivank replied.

'Keep believing it isn't real until the auction ends. Remember. This is your dream. These franchise tournaments are half won at the auction table.'

Cheeku spoke at length and somehow reined Vivank in to the other world.

'Teams have a purse of ₹5 crore with which you can buy up to 14 players today apart from the maximum of four outstation players you have already signed. You also need to accommodate your outstation players within the purse of ₹5 crore. Here we go with the first player of the day,' cried Ramsay as he pulled out the first player to be auctioned.

'Sameer Saxena it is! The current Indian superstar! With a base price of ₹1 crore!' announced Ramsay

'1.05,' bid Vivank.

'1.1,' the Titans bid.

'1.15,' Vivank raised.

'1.2,' the Titans weren't giving up.

'1.25.'

The Titans went up to 1.5, then the Hawks made entry!

'And you said they won't bid much as no one is sure of his availability!' Cheeku made a dig.

'Your call entirely!' Ricky gave Vivank a free hand.

Vivank kept bidding and finally got Sameer for ₹1.95 crore.

First player bought, but two fifth of the money lost already!

'Never mind! We got the superstar! Go by your instinct,' Pravi too was supportive.

The Dragons didn't or rather couldn't bid for other superstar players, as they had broken their bank with the very first player. The teams were soon busy shopping other players.

'The next player up for auction is Tariq Ahmed,' announced Ramsay.

'I want him surely,' whispered Vivank to his team.

'Don't bid initially then. Wait and bid at the end,' suggested Ricky.

So, they decided to wait on Tariq and make their bids at the end.

Tariq who started with a base price of ₹0.8 crore was at ₹2 crore with the bids with the Hurricanes.

'2.05,' Vivank slowly raised the paddle without inspiring much confidence as he clearly knew that 2.05 crores was beyond their estimates. But Vivank wanted Tariq and he made the bid.

'Sold,' announced Ramsay striking the hammer firmly on the table.

Vivank almost buried his head under the table after making what was perceived as an extremely overrated buy. None of his team mates at the table said anything. Not even a handshake! The Dragons had just blown away ₹4 crore on two players out of a total purse of ₹5 crore.

Vivank couldn't buy anyone else from his wish list other than Tony. He had to contend himself with lesser-known players, with base prices of ₹3 lakh and ₹5 lakh. Vivank just ensured that they picked a squad that covered all the skill sets including top order, middle order and lower order batting, wicket keeping, spin and fast bowling departments.

It was an action-packed day as all the teams picked their players. Nobody even had a moment for anything else other than the auction. Every time Vivank took his phone out, Cheeku would grab it and tell him to focus on the auction.

'With this we come to the end of today's proceedings,' declared Ramsay as he summarized the squads one final time.

Teams had already started discussing the favourites, dark horses and underdogs as they started to leave the auction room.

'Only three players from the list! So much for all the planning,' Ricky laughed looking at Vivank's list.

'These auctions are unpredictable! And tournaments are not won based on lists or paper, but by the fight the players put up on the field,' Vivank replied.

'Let's hope for the best!' said an optimistic Pravi, while Cheeku was busy counting the number of likes he had received for his 'mic drop' photo.

Vivank rushed to his room and dialled Leepa's number again.

It was ringing. Vivank's heartbeat was synchronous with the ring of the telephone.

'Finally, today is the day! She got back to me! Or has she?' thousand bells were ringing in Vivank's mind.

'Hello?' a grumpy male voice answered the phone.

'Hello this is Vivank, I want to speak to Leepa,' Vivank couldn't hide his emotions.

'She is resting now. Call tomorrow,' he replied.

'But! Can I please talk now?' Vivank pleaded.

'No,' came the stern reply.

'Where is she now?' asked Vivank.

'Galaxy Hospital, Ghaziabad,' the man replied. And before Vivank could ask another question, the man on the other end hung up the phone.

Vivank tried texting every possible romantic line, but not a single message went through.

'Only single tick. See, here.' He showed his phone to Cheeku.

Was it the end or was it another beginning? Vivank couldn't solve the Leepa puzzle yet!

∞

'It's this part of the auction that I was waiting for!' exclaimed a visibly thrilled MM, as he entered the party along with Billu and Ricky.

The team owners, a few superstar cricketers, members from the business and Bollywood fraternity had gathered for the 'after-auction' party at the same hotel.

There was booze, there were escorts and of course there was powder! Lots of it. The entire place was filled with sound and sleaze.

Vivank walked in and sat in a corner, quietly looking at the proceedings.

'Do you want dope?' an African man sat beside him.

'What is it? Powder?' Vivank asked spontaneously

All buried thoughts and skeletons came tumbling back. Ecstatic thoughts, that he had once experienced started creeping in again.

'No! Not just powder. This is "Golden Snow".' The man opened a small box and showed Vivank. Inside there were glittering golden coloured granules, shaped like snowflakes.

'See! Doesn't it look like golden snow?' the man asked in an seductive tone.

Vivank sheepishly nodded.

'It has 20 times the power of the usual powder and elevates you to an all-new level! Wanna try some?' he offered Vivank.

Vivank put his hand out, but saw Leepa's image all over the place. On the carpet, on the windows and on the chandeliers. Leepa was everywhere!

'No!' Vivank said in a sharp tone and walked away to his room. For once in his life, Vivank had done the right thing by saying no to the wrong thing. And for the first time his mind and heart were in unison.

Vivank wasn't feeling desperate anymore. He was feeling content and happy as he walked back to his room.

He had tears in his eyes, but Vivank felt two emotions—the love in his heart for Leepa and the fire in his belly to be a champion again!

Cheeku who was watching all this also gave a teary eyed, broad smile.

CHAPTER 12

A Tale of Three Hospitals

It was 6 a.m. and the sun was already blazing through the streets of Mumbai. Zia had just woken up and was wondering if it was day or night. The sharp and periodic beep from the heart rate monitor was the only sound that she could hear. And the archetypal scent of Iodoform was what she could distinctly smell. She could feel sharp pain all over her body owing to the multiple bruises that she had suffered. Her left leg was still in excruciating pain despite all medical interventions. She could barely feel her leg except for the pain radiating from it. She was in the hospital after being run over by the car being driven by MM and Ricky.

Just then, the doctor came in for his morning rounds and started examining her.

'You are getting better, like I said yesterday. The wounds are healing but your left leg still requires considerable amount of attention. A fracture on the ankle and a hamstring tear with multiple deep lacerations. Only these things are holding you back.'

'How long will they continue to hold me back, doctor?' Zia asked.

'A few more weeks at least,' the doctor replied.

'That's too long doctor, I have work to do!' Zia tried to convince the doctor.

'Well, all of us have work to do! Take it easy, ma'am. Sometimes, we need to listen to our body,' said the doctor with a smile.

Zia was not in the mood to listen to the doctor's advice.

'How is my colleague Himanshu, doctor? Is there any improvement?' Zia asked with a lot of concern, yet thinking about her possible next move already.

'Well, your friend is not as fortunate as you are! He took the brunt of the accident and is still not out of danger. His vitals are stable, but we need to monitor him closely as he suffered a head injury and multiple fractures. He will continue to be in the intensive care unit until there's any significant improvement,' the doctor walked off to the next room.

Zia pulled out her phone for the first time since the accident.

She started browsing through her messages for any update on MM and company. MM had won that round but Zia was in no mood to give up despite her setback. She angrily put aside the text Commissioner Tiwary had sent her. The message was an advisory asking her to be careful, mind her own work and routine duties. He reminded her of the enquiry that she was already facing and how her own life was under threat.

'Is that advice or a threat?' she asked herself.

She then checked an unread text sent by Karan, her informer. Karan had texted her that he had managed to get information about Femi and would visit her with the details once she was well.

She called Karan without wasting any time.

'Good morning, ma'am,' Karan answered the phone.

'Good morning, Karan. What's the update on Femi?' asked Zia.

'He was taken to Citylife Hospital in Dadar, ma'am. They had apparently removed the bullet from his leg before getting him to the hospital. The doctors found bullet traces in the leg in the operation theatre and had informed Dadar West police station. Sensing trouble he was removed from the hospital immediately after he stabilised,' replied Karan.

'Did you check the hospital records?'

'No use, ma'am. All false details from them,' replied Karan.

'Then how are you sure that it was Femi?' asked Zia.

'I got footage from the hospital cameras. His physical features matched with those in the database that you gave us, ma'am,' Karan added.

'Where's the footage now?' Zia asked. Suddenly her listless life had become eventful again. Except that she was still in the hospital and her body was still not ready for action.

'It's with me, ma'am!'

'Fine. Bring it to the hospital as soon as possible.'

'Sure, ma'am.'

After quickly reading the other messages, feeling relieved that she had a fresh lead, Zia caught up with everything she had missed in the world of Candy Crush. She was engrossed in no time, as her time in the hospital ticked away.

∞

'I feel pukish,' cribbed Vivank as he got out of the cab.

'Wow! How awesome of you to feel pukish when you finally get to meet your girlfriend after so many years! Nobody like you, seriously,' laughed Cheeku. 'And girlfriend or ex-girlfriend, we'll see soon enough,' he corrected himself.

They were standing in the reception of Galaxy Hospital. Vivank was feeling pukish because he had not slept the whole of the previous night and hadn't had any breakfast either. All he had in mind was Leepa. With Leepa came love and happiness, but with Leepa also came all the bad memories of the break-up. Images from that fateful day in Goa kept popping up in his mind making him weak and confused. He had given up all such nefarious habits now, but he wondered whether Leepa would accept him again. Such thoughts had filled his mind all through the night. He was about to get an answer to all his questions.

'Who is that guy who spoke on the phone? Why are his messages not going through? Why is she in the hospital now? What if her husband or boyfriend opens the door now?' Vivank kept thinking as they moved towards the counter.

'Leepa Azam,' Cheeku replied when he was asked the patient's details.

'Oh! Leepa Madam! She is in Room 183. First floor,' said the woman at the reception.

'You seem familiar with the name?' a curious Cheeku asked.

'Ya, she has been here for more than two years now. Don't you know?' the receptionist replied.

Now Cheeku kept quiet and they both started walking up.

Vivank became teary eyed as soon as he heard that she had been in the hospital for more than two years. He didn't really know what was coming up next or what was about to hit him. He was preparing himself to withstand any shock but this huge spectrum of uncertainty was making it very difficult for Vivank to cope. He felt numb and walked in silence.

Cheeku tried to pat his back and even made a couple of poor jokes as they walked together to the room, but Vivank didn't even hear them. Finally, they reached the first floor and stood outside Room 183. Cheeku rang the bell and stood still. Vivank stood behind Cheeku with his heart in his mouth.

An elderly man in his 60s opened the door. He was Leepa's father. Vivank recognised him. But he didn't seem to recognise either of them.

'Who are you?' He asked bluntly.

'I'm Cheeku and this is Vivank. We've come to see Leepa,' said Cheeku.

The man reluctantly let them in.

'We tried speaking to you over the phone yesterday but there was some signal problem, I guess,' Cheeku tried to strike a friendly chord with the man, but in vain. The man just ignored Cheeku's words and took them to the adjacent room.

Vivank saw Leepa lying on the bed listening to music. By her bedside was a bearded man in his 20s who was sharing the earphones with Leepa. Her mother was sitting at the other end of the room and was reading something.

'Who is this guy?' was Vivank's first question.

Leepa noticed him and her face erupted in the broadest possible smile. She unplugged the earphones and tried to sit up on the bed. The guy sitting by her side helped her sit up.

'I think, I asked who this guy is!' Vivank shouted now.

'Hey! Come on…' Leepa's smile grew even bigger.

'Okay. We need to talk,' she told Vivank and looked at her father. Her mother had stopped reading by now. They both reluctantly left the room. She then signalled the other guy to also leave the room.

'When women say "we need to talk", it simply means war,' Cheeku cheekily whispered to Vivank and walked out stealthily.

'What are you going to say about that guy?' Vivank started.

'You idiot! We haven't spoken for years! I have been rotting in this hospital for more than two years. All you care is about that guy? He is my brother!' answered Leepa.

'But you said you don't have a brother?' asked a perplexed Vivank.

'Yes, I did. He is my cousin and he's getting married in a couple of weeks which is why he is in Delhi. Now, will you please ask something about me?' Leepa said in an irritated tone.

'I'm sorry, I'm really sorry. I love you, truly do love you. I have made mistakes. Please forgive me for that. I'm over all that now and have become a better person. I'll never leave you in my life, no matter what happens!' Vivank spoke his heart out.

Both of them were in tears. He came and sat by her and held her hands. They just sat there for the next 10 minutes without speaking a word, just looking into each other's eyes.

'You remember what I had told you when you asked what I would do if we broke-up?' Leepa asked, clearing her throat.

'Yeah. You said you will never break-up at any cost,' replied Vivank.

'And if I did?' asked Leepa.

'If you did, you said you will jump off a building and die,' Vivank said recollecting their conversation.

'I did just that!' replied Leepa.

'Oh my god! What sort of a fool are you? I know you are an emotional and an impulsive person but who would do such a thing?' Vivank started palpitating.

'I am and always have been true in my love. I had absolute faith and commitment in us, for us! I may be foolish but I'm brutally honest!' she replied.

'What happened? Please tell me. I want to know all of it,' Vivank couldn't contain himself.

'Initially, I was very angry. Felt cheated. I was very impulsive and left Mumbai. Changed my number, deactivated all my social media handles. Got myself transferred to Delhi and started working here. In a couple of weeks, I realised that my entire life was only woven around you and I couldn't take a single step forward. I tried calling you but couldn't reach you. I didn't have Cheeku's number. I was extremely frustrated, depressed and emotional one night and remembered the word that I gave you,' continued Leepa.

'And then?' asked an anxious Vivank.

'And then what? Boom kaboom!'

'Holy crap! This is insane!' Vivank couldn't believe what he was hearing. He was feeling unbelievably guilty now.

'I'm sorry… Please forgive me.' He touched her feet and kissed them.

'Oh my god! I'm truly feeling happy after ages!' she said tearfully, continuing her story.

'I suffered multiple injuries and was in a coma until a few months ago. Then slowly, I clawed my way back to reality and started my rehab. Thankfully no major damage except that I have lost a couple of years in between!' she spoke.

'Why didn't you call me earlier?'

'Well, like I said, I came out of the coma only a few months back.'

'You could have called once you were out of the coma.'

'I could have, but I had my own reasons.'

'Like what?'

'I still wasn't sure about the whole thing and if I should get back to you. I couldn't take my mind off you for the past few months and then I finally decided. And I wasn't sure about your status either. But something kept telling me that we will be together,' she replied.

'I'm really sorry for everything. We've lost a few years, but we're not living even a day without each other for the rest of our lives,' Vivank said and hugged her emotionally.

∞

'This is the hard disk, ma'am,' Karan showed the footage to Zia, as promised.

'Play it on the laptop,' said Zia handing him the laptop.

They both viewed the footage involving Femi. He was brought in by two African men both of whom were unknown to Zia.

'That guy, the one getting admitted is Femi, the other two I'm not sure about,' she said.

They had two sequences of them entering and leaving the hospital.

'Zoom in… Zoom in…Zoom into the bag that the guy with Femi is carrying,' she urged.

'There… stop! Did you see that? Bag clearly shows the Emerald Group hotel's logo,' Zia said.

'Yes, ma'am!' Karan nodded.

'This bag is there on both the footage. I have a strong hunch about the hotel. How many Emerald Group hotels are there in the city?' she asked.

'They have three hotels, ma'am,' replied Karan.

'Get the check-in and check-out details of all the three emerald hotels of last one month and look out for any Africans who have checked in. Also, try to get the camera footage from these three hotels on the day they left the hospital,' ordered a confident Zia.

'What's the word on MM?' she asked.

'There is a huge buzz doing the rounds about a new and a very powerful addictive substance, ma'am. It's being called "Golden Snow" in the circles. Looks like it has become a rage since the

MSL after-auction party, which MM also attended,' Karan said.

'Hmmm.' Zia didn't say much. She started thinking and was thinking deep.

No matter how weak she was physically, she was still mentally very strong. In fact, stronger than she ever had been!

CHAPTER 13

Building Blocks

Dongri Dragons:

1. Sameer (captain/top-order batsman)
2. Tariq (all-rounder)
3. Bhupinder (opener/outstation player)
4. Vinayak (opener)
5. Pranav (top-order batsman/opener)
6. Tushar (middle-order batsman/wicket-keeper)
7. Tony (middle-order batsman)
8. Rajawat (left-arm spinner/outstation player)
9. Sharad (fast bowler)
10. Vinit (fast bowler)
11. Uday (off spinner)
12. Irfan (fast bowler/outstation player)
13. Nikhil (middle-order batsman)
14. Rohan (fast bowler)

'This is the official team list. This is the squad we could put together with the available purse. I know this squad is wafer thin without a great deal of back up, but having tracked each of them I still believe that we have a team that could fight its way up. They are all assembling at the RKM school ground today evening. We have a conditioning camp for one week before we begin the first match against the Hawks,' Vivank briefed Ricky and Pravi before going ahead with his full-time assignment.

News from Galaxy Hospital was that Leepa could go home in another week or so, and Vivank was extremely chuffed with the way things had turned around in his life. One thing that stood as the obstacle was success. He had never tasted lasting success in his personal or professional life. This upcoming tournament could give him that brilliant start towards that lasting success in his professional life. Vivank understood its importance and would leave no stone unturned to achieve it. He was all pumped up as he walked into the player's changing room at the stadium.

All the players had gathered across the room and were waiting for Vivank. All but Tariq and Sameer. Sameer had informed them that he would join them on the last day and apparently Tariq had told his personal trainer to inform him once the coach came and the meeting started.

All the others were eagerly looking forward to their new team and their coach. They had already had an ice-breaking session among themselves.

'I'm Vivank. Your coach, guide and friend at Dongri Dragons. It isn't going to be a typical top-down coach-player relationship. We all make mistakes and we learn from them. I have also made mistakes but the important thing is that I would frankly admit to them and I have learnt from them. If you could also admit and learn from your mistakes, along with some hard work and teamwork, I'm sure that we will do well. Our captain may not be joining us until the last day of our camp…'

'Hi Vivank! Good evening!' Tariq barged in, pulled up a chair and sat next to Vivank.

Vivank just nodded and continued his speech.

'In the coming days, we will devise specific roles for each of you based on your skill set and get you all accustomed to it and match ready. Cheeku will be my assistant and analyst. He will be helping you with your stats, videos and performance indicators. Our physio and trainers Sam and Ram are also with us. I strongly urge you not to hold back any injury or even a niggle. Discuss these things without delay with the physio. Physio and trainer have a separate session tomorrow morning, followed by a session by Cheeku focussing on your strengths and weaknesses,' Vivank concluded and walked them to the nets.

Everyone in the squad except Sameer and Tony were very young. Ranging from 16 to early the 20s. They were extremely fit, and more importantly, were a dedicated bunch who were willing to work hard and play as a team.

'So coach! What's up?' Tariq came and stood by Vivank.

'Hi Tariq. We are waiting to see you perform. Now go pad up!' Vivank spoke in a polite tone.

'Hey coach, it isn't done that way. You know I'm the next big thing in Indian cricket,' Tariq spoke with a careless tone.

'Ya Tariq, I know that and I do realise that, which is why we went all out for you at the auction,' Vivank replied.

'Yeah! But don't expect me to attend every session, and to bat and bowl whenever you wish to at the nets. You should understand that I do have a lot of endorsements and commercial commitments before the main season commences. So, I suggest you give me that freedom in the team so that I can light up the MSL. These leagues need superstars like me to spin money more than the kids playing there,' Tariq replied.

Vivank was just replaying in his mind how he had squandered auction money to buy Tariq. Cheeku looked at him from the adjacent nets and they both understood the situation and smiled without uttering a word.

'If it's freedom that you want, then so be it. List out your commercial commitments and give me your schedule in writing. I need you to have at least three full sessions with the bat and ball before you take field for the first match. You can fix those sessions according to your schedule. Like every other player in the team your performance counts more than your reputation. You will be dropped. I repeat you will be dropped if you don't perform for the team,' Vivank spoke in a firm voice looking straight into Tariq's eyes.

Tariq just gave a sarcastic smile and left.

The rest of the team toiled hard for the next few hours. Bhupinder was smacking quite a few balls out of the park, while Tony and Pranav looked steady. Irfan was finding it difficult to adjust to the new settings and was spraying the ball all over the pitch. Rajawat was continuously bowling some unplayable deliveries.

'They are much better than I had expected. Some of them are brilliant. I'm particularly impressed with Vinit, Rajawat and Bhupinder,' Cheeku told Vivank later.

'I didn't see much of Vinit today. Is he better than Irfan?' Vivank asked.

'I think so. He looks more consistent and steadier. Irfan was wayward today. I need to show him his pitch map and have a word with him tomorrow. But overall, when we see, these boys may not be proven match-winners or superstars but they are good. Very good,' Cheeku said.

'Imagine Sameer joining this team!' Vivank sounded excited.

'Hope he isn't another Tariq. He could have at least shown his face today. I know he is your good friend but still…' Cheeku put forth his apprehensions.

'No no, I don't think Sameer will be like Tariq. Plus, he is currently playing for India. Must be difficult to get a break, let him enjoy his break and come on the last day. Now let me enjoy my video call with Leepa!' Vivank said happily.

∞

Tears rolled down Zia's cheek involuntarily with every step that she took. The pain in her left leg, despite all the painkillers, was excruciating. She somehow had the mad will power to stand up on her own and get on track in pursuit of MM and company. She was just entering Hotel Imperial, located at Khar. It was about a week back that she had met Karan at the hospital and told him to check out the details pertaining to Femi and his friends. After a few days Karan had confirmed that Femi and his friends had gone to the hotel directly from the hospital. But all of them had checked out a few days ago.

'How I wish I had Himanshu to help me out,' she murmured to herself as she limped her way across the hotel lobby to the reception with the help of her crutch. She knew she was too late and her prey had given her the slip already.

'You are right, ma'am! Mr John and his friends checked-out last Tuesday. They were staying here for about a month,' the receptionist replied.

'Okay give me all their bill copies. I need bills of all the four rooms that they had stayed in,' Zia asked.

'Sorry ma'am, we are a premier hotel chain and these things are against our customer service policy,' the receptionist spoke in an uncooperative tone.

'See I have told you who I am. I have also shown you my ID card. It's of utmost importance and don't play the fool with me,' Zia warned him.

'Well ma'am... Err...'

Zia was holding him by the scruff of the neck before he could say anything.

Two minutes later...

'Here they are, ma'am,' he printed out and gave all their bill copies, neatly put in a folder.

Zia pulled up a chair and was going through them for some clue that could lead her forward.

'Good evening, sir, we have a courier for Dr Craig Langer, Room Number 204,' said the courier boy.

'How many times have I told you not to barge in like this,' shouted the manager rather curtly at the courier boy.

'Sorry sir,' he apologized in a shaken voice.

'Give it to me. I will give it to him,' the manager said.

'No sir! We are supposed to hand over the parcel to the client directly and get their signatures,' the boy reverted.

'He is our guest only, give it to me,' the manager insisted.

'No sir, our client policy doesn't allow us...'

'Okay wait, I'll talk to him,' the manager started dialling his phone.

'There is a courier for Dr Langer. What should I do? Okay... Okay...Will do,' manager hung up after speaking.

'Okay, here is the delivery address. Dr Langer, c/o Sibu Swamiji, Sibu Swamiji Ashram, Pantheon Park Enclave, Navi Mumbai. He will pay you the extra charges,' the manager explained.

Zia dug into her crutch and got up as fast as she could and walked up to them.

'Who is this Dr Langer? You said he is a hotel guest but you gave some other address to reach him. What is all this?' She spoke in an aggressive tone, gesturing with her hands towards him.

By then the manager had started trembling. 'I don't know anything ma'am. He is a famous pharmacological researcher from Australia. Last month he came here for a conference and has stayed here since then. For the past two weeks, he hasn't been seen much in our hotel. His things are still there, he comes and goes randomly. He had just given a contact number to get in touch in case of an emergency. When I called on that number now, somebody else picked up and gave me this address,' the manager said, still shaking visibly.

'Take me to Room 204, the one he's been using,' Zia ordered.

The manager tried resisting politely, but in vain. He put Zia onto his general manager, to whom Zia gave the same orders in a sterner manner.

'Don't waste my time. Just do as I say,' was her last words.

Five minutes later…

After more pleading and rule stating, when the manager realized he had no choice left, he led Zia to Dr Langer's room.

Five minutes ago…

The house keeping person hurriedly entered Room 204 and started pulling out some papers. He was doing a thorough check of the room, gathering pieces of paper and a mobile phone and putting them in his pocket.

As Zia and the manager were slowly walking towards the room, he ensured that he had collected all that he needed. He hurriedly made the bed and brought in fresh towels, toiletries and got out of the room, just as Zia and the manager were walking out of the elevator. They opened the door and got into the room. Meanwhile, the housekeeping guy quickly walked out using the service lift along with his housekeeping trolley. He took the emergency exit and walked out of the hotel with the papers. Outside the hotel he removed his cap, spectacles and beard and got into the car where his friend Billu was waiting. His name was Ricky and he had successfully completed his job for the day!

'I realised something was wrong when I noticed that the towel and toiletries in the room hadn't been placed properly. The bedspread wasn't tucked in neatly either, everything was done rather hurriedly. This is the reason,' Zia told the manager. Her finger pointed to Ricky from one of the windows as Ricky got into the car.

CHAPTER 14

Insights

'Sameer Saxena is here!' There was huge buzz around the cricket ground. People from outside had turned in to just catch a glimpse of their cricketing idol. The entire team was ready to see their captain and the superstar and play alongside him. Irfan and Vinit stopped bowling in the nets and were waiting for Sameer to walk in. Bhupinder meanwhile was trying to hit those sixes, so that Sameer would watch and appreciate him. Tariq had just finished his mandatory third batting session, before the first match, and was walking out of the nets. He was feeling extremely insecure about Sameer.

'He might be the present but I am the future,' Tariq thought to himself as he counted the exact number of selfies Sameer posed for as he walked towards the nets.

'Hi Sameer bhai!' Tariq ran towards Sameer and hugged him, still cursing Sameer in his head. Then Tariq quietly walked off the ground.

Sameer gave him a customary hug, said a brief hi and went to the nets.

Sameer repeated the same hug-hi sequence with Vivank. By then the entire squad had gathered around him.

'Hi all! Awesome seeing you all here. Let's rock the tournament. See you all tomorrow for the match!' Sameer announced.

And he started walking back. He then turned back suddenly and called out to Vivank.

'Vivank, you'll brief me about the players half an hour before the match tomorrow,' he said snapping his fingers and then walked off.

There was deafening silence among the entire squad who had been waiting for their hero to turn up for practice for so long. To bowl at him, to train with him and to play with him were things that they were expecting. Disappointment was the mildest word to describe their feelings. The entire team's morale tanked, which made Vivank give them a pep talk to raise their spirits.

Cheeku kept imitating Sameer's 'snap' and irritating Vivank the whole evening!

Vivank felt betrayed. He had made the team splurge almost the entire purse on two players and neither of them were synchronising with the team. He wouldn't be worried about performance issues, but these attitude issues seemed beyond his control. He was getting worried that things were beyond repair. No matter what, he wanted to be honest with himself and promised to back his decisions.

He gathered the remaining players and gave them another long talk after the practice session, on the eve of the first match and followed it by a fun-filled truth or dare round, sitting on the lush green outfield in a huge circle with the players.

The players were back to being their happy selves at the end of it and walked away from the ground with a lot of positivity.

It was match day as the MSL officially kicked off. There was hype around Mumbai as the organisers had left no stone unturned with their promotions. Live television telecast across the country and web streaming made MSL a trending event on and offline.

'Welcome to Match 2 of the MSL. It's Andheri Hawks taking on Dongri Dragons. We are live from the RKM cricket ground for what is touted to be a clash between India Titans Kiran Shah who is leading the Hawks and Sameer Saxena leading the Dragons. The toss is just a few minutes away, as the players warm up in the outfield,' the commentator announced.

'It's amazing to see how this ground has been transformed in the last few months. Kudos to the Dragons' "management",' praised the organisers as well as the commentary team on air.

Vivank had just finished briefing Sameer about the team members, reluctantly. He also went through the bowlers in detail and put forth his views on which bowler should be bowling which over. Sameer interrupted at every second line and checked his phone, which frustrated Vivank even more.

'Don't worry, he will take care of things on the field,' Cheeku tried to cheer up Vivank.

'Let him take care of things on the field but he should get to know his players first,' Vivank was cribbing to Cheeku as Sameer went out for the toss.

Sameer won the toss and elected to field first.

'Ya ya sure. Towards the end of this match, I'll fake an injury and walk out. Won't be playing this tournament any more. My contract says I'll get full payment, if I turn up and play at least one match. So, you go ahead and book the tickets for London. I'll take care of things here,' Sameer hung up the phone, placed it in his locker and walked to the field, 'leading' his team!

Vivank nervously stood at the boundary line with Irfan. Irfan wasn't playing the game as only two outstation players were allowed, with Bhupinder and Rajawat doing extremely well in the warmup games, it was very difficult to drop them. Also, Vivank thought that Irfan needed some more time to be 'match ready'.

'Your time will come Irfan. Make it count,' he patted Irfan's shoulders as the match began.

The Hawks made 166/6 in their 20 overs, thanks to a swashbuckling 72 off 41 balls from their captain Kiran Shah. For the Dragons, Rajawat bowled superbly picking four wickets. Vinit and Rohan were steady with their seam bowling. Tariq picked a wicket but was a touch too expensive.

Dragons lost Vinayak early but Bhupinder and Sameer kept them going. Bhupinder was playing extremely well and impressed everyone with his flamboyant shots. Needless to mention, Sameer, was easily scoring runs and the two plundered the Hawks' bowling attack. Tariq, meanwhile, was padded up and secretly hoping for one of his team mates to get out. So, that he could go in next. Unfortunately, that wasn't to be, as both Sameer with 78 not-out and Bhupinder with 71 not-out, finished the game for the Dragons in 16 overs. The Dragons had won their first game emphatically. Vivank pumped his fists in relief more than jubilation. Leepa who was watching on TV was pumping her fists in jubilation too. Cheeku, meanwhile, was busy looking for his Instagram moments.

'Good job, Vivank. Clinical win,' Pravi shook hands with Vivank.

'Well done coach saab,' Ricky patted Vivank and then went around wishing the players.

Sameer limped off the field and was visibly limping in the dressing room and during the presentations.

'I think I'm injured, coach. Will let my medical team assess my condition and let you know,' he told Vivank as he left the ground.

One hour later Ricky, Pravi and Vivank received a mail.

It read:

> During today's MSL matches between the Dragons and Hawks, it looks like Mr Sameer Saxena has injured his left calf muscle, which most probably looks like a tear. He requires further medical attention, follow up and rehab. At this juncture, he will not be able to train or play for the next four weeks.

It was from Sameer's medical team.

'₹2 crore for the 78 runs that he scored today. It amounts to ₹2,56,410 per run!' Cheeku said looking at his computer.

Vivank had mixed feelings. He was feeling bad about his decision to pick Sameer and how his decision affected the team composition now. At the same time, he was happy that the rest of the team was shaping-up well.

'Don't worry about the financial aspects. I'll talk to the management. The team is doing well, let's keep going. Tariq will be captain now?' Ricky asked.

'No! Tony will be captain. He is experienced and is a team man. Tariq is too selfish,' Vivank explained.

'Right! Your call it is!' Ricky endorsed.

Vivank walked into the team huddle in the dressing and announced Tony as their new captain.

∞

'My team has won! One more reason to celebrate!' MM was adding ice to his glass of whiskey. Billu too, was drinking gleefully.

'Just like you had predicted, the response to "Golden Snow" has been amazing, MM bhai. You are a genius,' Billu clapped as he spoke.

MM had newly modified a bike into a seat on which he sat and drank. He was 'classily' sitting there and drinking while Billu was sitting on a bike tyre, which had been modified into a seat.

'I heard that that police scumbag is out of the hospital now. Injured, yet she is lurking around. Be careful with her. Hope Femi is safe. He is an important part of our global supply chain,' MM spoke in a cautious tone.

'Yes, bhai. Femi is in a safe place. Him and his friends vacated the hotel too. I told him not to make unnecessary calls to anyone and to just concentrate on the work,' Billu replied.

'Okay. I've sent a note to colonel too, informing him about the happenings,' MM said.

'Oh! What did colonel say, bhai?' Billu asked.

'He already had the news that the stupid hotel manager had told stupid things to the scumbag. So, he has cleared out everything himself! He also knows that the scumbag suspects Dr Langer and the ashram is his address,' MM said without any inhibition.

Soon he switched to his funny, cautious tone again, 'We'll have to be careful about Femi and about the ashram because that will be the next place she'll visit!' said MM cautiously, as he gulped down his drink!

∞

'Swamiji's ashram will be the first place where he would expect me to go, especially after I checked out Dr Langer's room the other day,' Zia spoke to Himanshu sitting by his hospital bed in the ICU.

Himanshu had regained consciousness a day back and was just

about out of danger. First thing he wished to know once he regained consciousness was about Zia's investigation. Zia was initially hesitant considering his health. But she herself couldn't resist talking about her investigation to her most trusted man. So, there she was detailing their cat and mouse game updates to Himanshu.

'So, what are you going to do? Are you going to go, ma'am?' Himanshu asked curiously, adjusting his pillow.

'No. I've already sent a person to check the ashram. There is nothing inside the ashram that would interest us. Not even Dr Langer,' Zia said confidently.

'What about the Swamiji of the ashram, ma'am?' asked Himanshu

'He isn't here. He is mostly travelling and hardly spends time in his ashram,' reverted Zia.

'Oh! So, we don't have any evidence that Swamiji is involved in all this, right ma'am?' asked a visibly disappointed Himanshu.

'Actually, we do have a lead. I have an informer who says he had spotted Swamiji with MM multiple times when MM was in Arthur Road jail!' Zia informed.

'Oh my god. Was Swamiji in jail? For what?' Himanshu's increased heart rate was visible on the machine.

'I don't have the data on that yet, but I've asked the jail authorities to provide me with the necessary information. But my source is very sure that Swamiji and MM were seen together many times, over a span of few months, in the jail,' Zia added.

By now Himanshu's pupils were dilated with excitement.

'Oh! This is getting interesting and intriguing ma'am! So, this Swamiji has been helping MM in his drug racket and is still helping him and his men. Am I correct, ma'am, to assume that?' asked an excited Himanshu.

'Yes. But we have been unable to uncover anything in the ashram or track this Swamiji or find out more about Dr Langer. Something doesn't connect,' Zia said.

'Oh! I'm sure you'll find it ma'am. Meanwhile, have you heard anything more about the colonel, ma'am?' asked Himanshu.

'No, nothing other than the fact that all my intel shows that colonel is the one controlling MM!' Zia said.

'So, Swamiji and colonel are the players running the show behind MM, isn't it ma'am?'

'Yes. And that is not all. You know what, there's a new product called "Golden Snow" in the powder market and MM seems to be invested in it. They are testing and circulating it at MSL matches,' Zia continued.

'Oh! If you are sure then we could take out an arrest warrant against MM, isn't it, ma'am?' asked Himanshu.

'For him to come out again of the jail and start something else? I want him dead by the end of it! Period,' claimed Zia.

'Hmmm. What do we know about this Golden Snow ma'am?' asked a curious Himanshu.

'It's supposed to be 20 times more powerful and effective than the routine powder. I have managed to get some samples from Femi and have sent them for forensic analysis,' informed Zia.

'Oh yes! I totally forgot! Was about to ask about Femi, ma'am. Were you able to track him to his hospital?' asked Himanshu.

'Haha! Tracked him from hospital to the hotel he stayed at, then found the numbers he used to call from his hotel bills and tracked down his address, a house-cum-warehouse near Mulund,' replied Zia.

'That's awesome ma'am! Were you able to get anything from him apart from that powder?' asked Himanshu.

'No! Nothing more than what I have interpreted so far,' replied Zia.

'I'm sure with such strong evidence he will be under your impregnable custody and unassailable interrogation by now,' added Himanshu.

'Nope!'

'He escaped ma'am?'

'Nope!'

'Then?'

'I had him killed some 30 minutes back!' replied Zia.

CHAPTER 15

Dragon Wars

'See there is this Swamiji who is deeply connected to MM and there is also this mysterious colonel who seems to have MM's back,' Zia looked slightly worried.

Himanshu was still in the hospital bed and Zia was sitting by his side.

'And we cannot track either of them, ma'am?' asked Himanshu.

'I wish we could. Everything at the ashram seems picture perfect and the guys who manage it don't seem to be giving anything away. If we go beyond the line, they'll start playing the religion card,' Zia replied.

'That everyone is doing these days ma'am. Both this religion and that religion!' Himanshu replied.

'Yeah, but we can't take that risk, right? And bring a bad label on the police force. As such there are so many labels that are already attached to us. And commissioner saab has already warned me and asked me to keep quiet. If I go after the ashram now, then…' Zia trailed off.

'Understood' ma'am. Our hands are tied. As always! But we will fight, ma'am. Even if our hands are tied!' Himanshu replied enthusiastically.

'I've already checked the fund receipts of the ashram. Needless to say, the ashram receives a lot of foreign funding. A whole lot of it. I've already reported this to the Enforcement Directorate for investigation into the money laundering aspects, but I feel there is definitely more to it than just money laundering,' Zia added.

'Why did Swamiji go to jail in the first place, ma'am?' Himanshu asked.

'Good question! The answer will surprise you! I went through the Arthur Road jail records. There is no record of Swamiji going to jail. I checked with our stations also, there is not a single FIR against Swamiji,' Zia informed.

'Oh my god. How is that possible, ma'am?' asked a confused Himanshu.

'Because Swamiji has never been booked or arrested,' Zia replied.

'But our trusted informer said he had seen MM with Swamiji often in jail,' Himanshu continued.

'Yes. What our informer said is also true,' Zia mentioned.

'Ma'am! Am I hearing things, right? I'm not sure about things after the accident. Yesterday my wife said the same,' Himanshu sounded confused.

'You are hearing things right Himanshu ji. I looked up newspaper reports during the time MM was in jail. And corroborated them with Swamiji's news. During that period, Swamiji had initiated an outreach meditation programme for the Arthur Road jail inmates. He himself had visited jail often and "taught" meditation to the inmates,' Zia clarified.

'Oh! now I get it, ma'am. Swamiji manipulated an outreach meditation programme so that he could often meet MM in private and share something important,' Himanshu replied.

'Yes!' Zia confirmed.

'What the hell do you think about yourself?' Tariq furiously asked Vivank.

'How does that matter to you?' Vivank asked.

'Because my value is not fully realised in this team, thanks to the way you think,' Tariq hit the furniture in the dressing room with his bat as he spoke.

'Now calm down. Whatever decision is taken, is taken in the best interest of the team. Given your other important commitments, I don't know if you will be able to invest completely in the team. Also, you need to become a better team player if you want all your dreams to really come true,' Vivank said.

'Oh! Thanks for your valuable lessons to make me a team player. Let me search for your face when I wear that blue jersey and play for the country next year at the world cup. I have already achieved more as a player than what you could ever achieve in your entire supposed career.' He threw the bat down and started to leave.

'Thanks for reminding me of that and good luck for your world cup dreams. But before that there is this city-based cricket league that you are supposed to play in. Better play that in the right spirit and perform,' Vivank spoke in a sharp tone.

'Else?' Tariq asked.

'Else, you'll be benched. Simple,' Vivank reverted.

The Dongri Dragons then played the Powai Puff boys and Colaba Kings. They won both those games and were sitting comfortably at the top of the table. Bhupinder scored heavily in both the games, which the Dragons won. With scores of 56 and 83 in those two matches, Bhupinder was sitting at the top as the tournament's highest run scorer. The rest of the Dragons' batting order was largely untested because of Bhupinder's superlative performance. Tariq made a duck and a scratchy 40 off 60 deliveries, which almost cost his team the match. He never made much of an impression on the bowling front either. He kept thinking that he would topped the batting and bowling charts, if not for the way Vivank handled a superstar like him. Vineet and Rohan were making steady progress, keeping Irfan out of the playing 11 by the sheer virtue of their performance.

The Dragons played their fourth game against the Titans, who had won the toss and elected to bat first. They were considered as one of the strongest batting units in the tournament and they were living up to their reputation. The current national-level player Ritesh, who became the tournament's biggest star after Sameer's exit, was ripping the bowling attacks apart, making huge waves and was attracting humongous crowds to his matches.

As expected, Ritesh and his opening partner Amay took on the bowling attack of the Dragons and pulverized them all over the park. Eleven fielders were not enough for Tony to play with. Tony's bowlers were completely off colour. Tony, who seldom bowled, brought himself on to bowl at one stage, and he too was dished out the same treatment by Ritesh and Amay. The Titans made a mammoth 221/2 at the end of their designated 20 overs and Ritesh ended with a 138 not out, which propelled him to the top of the batting charts, pushing Bhupinder down.

All eyes were on Bhupinder as the Dragons began their chase. Unfortunately, though, the Dragons lost Bhupinder in the very first over and were never really in the chase as they kept losing wickets at regular intervals. Tariq alone played a selfish hand, remaining not— out till the end making 32 runs of 57 balls. The Dragons lost the game by 102 runs—the biggest loss by any team in the tournament so far.

'It's not just about the loss, it's always about the way we lost. What hurts most is that we gave up too soon, which is never acceptable. Champions don't give up. If you want to be champions, then don't give up,' Vivank tried his best in helping the team bounce back.

The Dragons for sure heard whatever Vivank had to say after their embarrassing loss to the Titans and fought valiantly in the next two games against the Hurricanes and the Powai Puff boys, but they lost both those games very narrowly. By five runs and three runs, respectively. The tournament was past its half-way stage and the Dragons were now in the middle of the points table. They had four matches remaining and they had to win at least two of them to qualify for the final.

What still looked like a manageable scenario for the Dragons turned into an uphill task in no time, because of the sudden Mumbai rains as their next two games against Hurricanes and Titans were washed off. The morale in the Dragon's camp was extremely low as their campaign had sunk from good to bad to worse.

Looking from the outside, with two to go and still in contention for a place in the finals was not really something many would have expected after their auction and after the league's biggest superstar Sameer pulled out. But the Dragons had managed to defy the odds to keep themselves at the top of the league for a while before slumping again. The critics and experts alike were in praise of Vivank for what he had done with such a young team, transforming them into a potential tournament winning unit. But the biggest question now was whether Vivank had it in him to bring them back from the brink of elimination and guide them into the finals. Will Vivank and Tony inspire a turnaround of the team's fortunes? This was the biggest question on the minds of all those who followed the MSL.

It was about 8 p.m. and it was still drizzling outside. Vivank had scheduled a team meeting and the entire team had gathered in the meeting hall. Vivank walked in, dressed in the Dragons' team attire and played a video.

The video started with a building being zoomed into, with a mild guitar tune running in the background. Vivank was shown in bed. Initially puking, getting treated, struggling to get up and even walk to the washroom. It then showed his journey back to health. Sitting with a group of people like him, listening to their talks, playing with tennis balls, then slowly getting back to his normal life—Vivank's treatment and rehabilitation programme was beautifully portrayed in the video. Most of the team members were teary eyed towards the end of the video. Some of the boys even wept aloud. The entire team got up, clapped and roared a cheer for the last segment, which showed Vivank being back to normal and slowly picking up his cricket bat again, and a tear from Vivank's eyes falling on the bat. The video ended with Vivank walking proudly onto the cricket field again with the bat in his hand.

'If I can be here from being there, then you all can achieve anything from where you are now. Nothing more to say. See you all tomorrow morning,' Vivank left the room, leaving everyone pumped up.

'It is easier to search for God than for hidden cameras!'

Zia was sitting in her office room and watching one of those famous speeches by Swamiji, peppered with his trademark humour.

'For a frequent and professional speaker, he pauses so much between each word,' Zia thought aloud.

There was a knock at the door and in came Karan.

'Here is the list of armed services personnel who have been court martialled in the last 10 years, ma'am. And here is the list of people discharged from duty in the armed forces in the last 10 years on medical grounds. It took a lot of effort and persuasion to get these, ma'am,' Karan spoke with a sense of accomplishment.

'Good. We have something to crack at,' replied Zia.

'Ma'am? I don't understand,' asked a perplexed Karan.

'There is an important "Colonel" who we need to track down,' Zia explained.

'Right, ma'am,' Karan replied.

'Here is the list of phone numbers which were in correspondence with Dr Langer's hotel room. Check if any of these numbers point to anyone of these people from the report you got from the armed forces,' Zia further explained.

'Wow! That's super cool ma'am! I think we are moving in the right direction,' Karan replied enthusiastically.

Zia gave a slight smile and went back to watching the Swamiji video.

∞

'Sure, you want this change?' Tony asked Vivank.

'Want what?' Vivank questioned back.

'Nikhil for Tariq?' Tony asked.

'Yeah skip. Tariq doesn't seem to mend his ways, has not made a single useful contribution thus far. What other option do we have? Besides, Nikhil has really been working hard and patiently been waiting for his turn,' Vivank reasoned out.

'That's all true. Accepted coach. But Tariq has been a proven match winner in the past and brings in a lot of experience. Also, by swapping in Nikhil for Tariq, we are losing out on a bowling option,' Tony said.

'Well, past counts for nothing, if you are not able to keep your present together. And the sixth bowling option if needed, is going to be you!' Vivank said. 'I have seen you bowl at crucial junctures and get wickets, only when you were out of batting form two seasons back you started concentrating more on your batting and started neglecting your bowling. This is the time to show your bowling prowess again,' he continued.

'Well, you saw it in the Titans game yourself. I did try it but was whacked all over the park. Not to mention the extras that I gave, unable to control the swing on the ball,' Tony said in a sad tone.

'That's exactly what I am talking about. Nobody can get it to reverse in this MSL circuit as much as you do. Just put more into bowling practice, you will be the team's biggest weapon when needed. And talking about combination, I do genuinely see you as an all-rounder. So technically speaking, you will replace Tariq as the all-rounder, and Nikhil will take your place as a middle order batsman,' Vivank said as they wrote out the playing 11 ahead of their penultimate match against the Colaba Kings.

Hearing the news of getting dropped, Tariq picked up his bag, foul mouthed Vivank and walked away from the ground right before the match. Pravi tried bringing him back but all her efforts were futile. Meanwhile, the game had started and Bhupinder was on a rampage. He struck his first century of the tournament and the

Dragons made 192/4 in 20 overs, with decent contributions from Nikhil and Tony. In reply, the Kings made a decent chase but were bundled out for 182. The Dargons had gotten their much-needed win, but they needed one more win to march into the finals.

Their final match came against the Hawks, against whom they had opened their campaign. Like they did in the first game, the Hawks captain Kiran Shah decided to bat first after winning the toss.

'Wow! Just what I had hoped for!' exclaimed a relieved Vivank from the dressing room seeing Hawks opting to bat first. This was their last game at the RKM school grounds. Continuous rains for two days before the match meant that the pitch was extremely damp. By now, Vivank knew their home pitch like the back of his hand and wanted his team to bowl first and exploit the pitch. Whatever Vivank had hoped for came true, as the Dragons' bowlers Vinit and Rohan rampaged the them batting order and Rajawat finished off their tail. The Hawks were bowled out for 91 in 18 overs, which the Dragons chased down quite easily.

The entire team was elated and ecstatic. They had won in grand style and were in the finals of the inaugural edition of the MSL, a feat that everyone would have discounted them of, a month ago. Vivank's boys were jubilantly running around and they had every reason to be so. The Dongri Dragons were on the covers of cricket magazines, on top of the regional social media trends. A few players had already started getting calls for brand endorsements. Rajawat was spoken of as the next big thing and Bhupinder was already in many of the experts' and fans' India squad for the next world cup. The Vivank success story was all over the media now, for a change.

Vivank though was unfazed with all the hype surrounding the

final. He had seen the lowest of the lows and was too numb now to react to the hype created for the final.

But there was one thing he was still excited about—Leepa.

Leepa was out of the hospital and was going to be with him for the finals. No matter how much he tried to underplay it, the thought of him winning in front of Leepa, let alone in front of the thousands of spectators on the ground and lakhs on television and the internet, made his heart flutter. His moment had finally come. Will he fully seize it?

It was around 6 a.m. Zia had just made some coffee and sat down with the newspapers. Beating the news of the MSL finals between the Titans and the Dragons was another tragic headline that had rocked Mumbai.

'MSL cricketer, Prathik, found dead in hotel room after suspected cocaine overdose,' was the main headlines in all the newspapers.

The newspaper report claimed that this could have been an effect of the after-match party and went on to repeatedly mention a new cocaine variant called Golden Snow that was now considered very popular in the market.

Zia called Himanshu immediately.

'Did you hear about Prathik?' asked Zia.

'Yes, ma'am. Cocaine overdose. MSL organisers are trying hard to cover up, giving other predisposing medical conditions as the cause of death. MM is putting pressure on the organisers too,' Himanshu replied.

'Did you check the forensic report?' asked Zia.

'Yes ma'am, report confirms the presence of about 6.5 grams of a cocaine-like drug in the circulatory system,' answered Himanshu.

'Oh my god! What is the usual amount present in overdose deaths?' asked a curious Zia.

'About 1.2–2 grams, ma'am!' Himanshu replied.

'Oh my....'

CHAPTER 16

Missing Pieces

Prathik's death had put the whole of Mumbai in a state of shock. It was the morning of the MSL final but the entire city was talking about Prathik.

'What is this Golden Snow?'

'These things happen all the time in celebrity parties, don't they?'

'Who all are involved in this?'

'Why is it that something dark almost always happens in these cricket leagues?'—were some of the questions being asked by most. Commissioner Tiwary was investigating the death and Zia was specifically instructed to stay away from this.

∽

'Yes, I have been asked to stay away from all of this and this is not the first time!' said Zia in a tone of mixed emotions. She was dressed in her pyjamas and tried to look relaxed but she wasn't. She hadn't slept all night and her eyes looked really drowsy.

Karan just stood listening to her, as obediently as ever.

'It means we dig deeper. But we don't have much time left. MM and company shouldn't get away again,' Zia added.

'Yes, ma'am,' Karan replied dutifully.

'Did you check the phone numbers from where Dr Langer got calls to his hotel room? Dr Langer has had this habit of not using a mobile phone. So, these phone numbers will surely help us. Especially, if they have some armed forces connection,' Zia added.

'Yes, ma'am. Got the point, but unfortunately I could find nothing suspicious in the list that we have,' Karan informed.

'Give me the list, let me see,' Zia asked.

Zia started running through the list repeatedly and gave a frustrated look.

She was about to hand over the paper to Karan but suddenly pulled it back.

'These three calls from Happy Travels!' Her eyes lit up.

'Yes, ma'am. Must have been for his ticketing. All three calls are of very short durations,' Karan informed.

'No! I'm sure that we have a lead here. I have seen quite a few of these "Happy Travels" calendars in photos of Swamiji's ashram that my guy clicked when he had gone there to check things out,' Zia informed.

'Oh!' Karan didn't see that coming.

'Now check the ownership and other details of this Happy Travels immediately,' Zia ordered.

∞

It took quite some effort from Vivank, Cheeku and the support staff to get the incident off the players' minds and put them on the field with the right frame of mind. The more Vivank dwelled on the recent tragedy, the scarier his own past seemed to him. It gave him a sudden chill down his spine to even think about it all again. He was lucky and fortunate to be where he was presently and thanked

God as he got down from the team bus for the grand finale of the MSL. The final was being held at the Wankhede Stadium. The dream of any Mumbai cricketer who begins playing at Shivaji Park or its surrounding bylanes is to ultimately play a match at the Wankhede. That dream was to come true for many young cricketers that night.

It was around 6.30 p.m. and a huge crowd had already gathered by the time Vivank walked into the stadium. The floodlights were on and the atmosphere was already electric. The skeletons of the Prathik incident were buried for now and the focus was on the game. Right outside the dressing room, Vivank saw Leepa.

'I was hoping and praying daily for this day,' said an emotional Leepa, still on wheelchair support.

'Doctor said you could walk. Why are you still on the wheelchair?' Vivank asked.

'I can walk small distances for now. Cannot climb stairs yet,' Leepa replied.

'Will you watch the match from here?' Vivank asked.

'No, I wish to watch from the stands. I want to soak in the whole atmosphere,' replied an enthusiastic Leepa.

Vivank pushed her wheelchair into the lift and then onto the stands. Pravi accompanied them along with a couple of Leepa's friends. On the way, Leepa pointed to the banners and posters that had Vivank's name and photos. Everything felt so surreal for Vivank.

'Here we go! The best seat in the house,' he made her sit there. Leepa pulled him close and planted a kissed on his forehead and gave a thumbs-up. Neither of them spoke, but they both knew exactly what the other had to say.

Pravi, deciding to watch the match with Leepa, patted Vivank and wished him luck. Vivank walked with full energy into the dressing room. Nobody was outside, all of them had gathered in a circle and had their faces turned inwards. None of the voices or the eyes, however, had anything encouraging to convey. A confused Vivank broke the circle and walked into it.

Bhupinder was in excruciating pain as the doctor was putting a sling around his right shoulder.

'He fell near the boundary ropes during the fielding drills and dislocated his shoulder,' said a visibly sad Cheeku.

They were 10 minutes away from the toss on the night of the big final and their best player was injured and ruled out of the game.

'Let's put Irfan in place of Bhupi. Let it be an opportunity to unleash Irfan on them. Unleash Irfan to the world,' Vivank told Tony.

'A bowler in place of a batsman? We will be a batsman short,' Tony asked in an unsure tone.

'Just imagine Bhupi got a duck tonight and play. I know it's a huge loss to the team and for Bhupi, but I'm sure he has made his mark already and bigger opportunities will definitely come by for him,' Vivank told the team in the huddle.

'Let's show them that the Dragons are not a one-man army! Let's show them that every one of us is a champion! We wanted to win the title for you coach, now let's win it for you and Bhupi,' said Vinayak.

Vivank had goosebumps by the time Vinayak finished.

'For coach and Bhupi!' they shouted in unison and strode onto their dugout.

Tony won the toss and the Dragons elected to bat first in the big final.

∞

'Happy Travels is registered in the name of Anand Bhatia, ma'am. But he isn't there at the company. All the operations of the travel agency are carried out by a man called Kumar.'

'What is the background of this Anand Bhatia?' Zia was clearly pondering something.

'I have not been able to track that ma'am. No one knows,'

'Great,' Zia's was slowly winning back confidence. 'I may actually be able to help you out. When did this travel agency start?' asked Zia.

'2005, ma'am,' replied Karan.

'Now take the court marshall and medical grounds discharge list from armed forces and look in the years 2004–05,' Zia mentioned.

'Ma'am! I can't believe my eyes. It's says Anand Bhatia was discharged on medical grounds in 2004,' an excited Karan replied.

'And what rank did he hold?' Zia asked.

'Colonel, ma'am,' pat came the answer.

∞

A few minutes later, Zia got a call from the hotel manager where Dr Langer had stayed.

'Yes, that would be great. Please send it to my mobile phone,' she said.

Karan could sense confidence and happiness in her voice. A stark difference from her confused tone in the morning.

'How quickly life changes if we wait patiently!' he thought to himself.

'Finally, Lady Luck is smiling on us,' she said after she hung up.

'What is it, ma'am? I'm really curious,' Karan asked.

'I had earlier asked the hotel to get more details about the calls made to Dr Langer's room. Luckily a call from Happy Travels has been recorded by a hotel intern for his training purpose,' Zia said.

'Those "your calls may be recorded for training purposes" have a use after all,' Karan laughed.

Zia had a beep on her phone then.

'Got it! Let me play it straight away,' said an excited Zia.

The voice recording started playing and the voice from Happy Travels told Dr Larger that he would meet him at the 'lab'.

'Is this Kumar's voice?' Zia asked.

'No, I spoke to Kumar just a few hours ago. This isn't his voice!' Karan answered confidently.

'It is the colonel's voice! Oh wait! Oh my god,' Zia paused her voice recording and played Swamiji's YouTube speech.

'Same voice, same long pause between words. It can only mean one thing,' added Zia.

'Ma'am. I can't believe this!' Karan simply couldn't believe what he was hearing, yet he knew that was the truth.

'Yes, Karan. Swamiji and colonel are one and the same. Anand Bhatia!' Zia concluded.

CHAPTER 17

Final Strokes

'What a fool I've been all these days! Everything I was looking for was right in front of my eyes and I had turned a blind eye to it all,' Zia was continuously blaming herself as her car was speeding outwards from the city on the road to Dongri. There were two more taxis behind her as well with six armed men in each of them. Karan, herself and the driver were in the jeep that was leading the way. Himanshu was on the mic from his bedside.

Zia kept looking at a map on her phone and was cursing herself for her inefficiency. 'The rock cliff and RKM school are at a walkable distance. 250 metres from the north gate to the cliff leads to the school. Yet we missed it,' she said.

Karan couldn't understand what she was trying to say. He was sitting quietly thinking about what it could be. Zia didn't care if Karan understood or not. She just wanted to lament.

They soon reached the spot where they had parked their cars near the school that day, when they had been runover by Ricky and MM. This time too they were in plain clothes, but were better armed and had more men at their disposal.

'All of you stay here and wait for my instructions. Karan and I are going in,' Zia gave clear instructions and started walking.

Every sight Zia saw there was haunting her. She was brutally hit by a car at that very place and here she was again at the same venue, once again flirting with danger.

'I've been so fortunate all my life, have escaped extremely dangerous situations but surely my luck has to run out sometime. Hope this is not the time. Hope, I live to see another day,' she was thinking as she successfully climbed over the school wall once again.

'Let's walk towards the building that would be closest to the northern gate of the rock cliff,' she told Karan, looking at her phone.

By then it was fully dark and it would have been difficult for anybody to spot them.

Zia and Karan walked past the newly constructed cricket ground that hosted all the Dragons home games. It wore a completely deserted look now, as all the action had shifted to the Wankhede Stadium.

Zia found the closest building and they got into a passage. At the end of the passage was a short figure who was apparently guarding the door. Zia instructed Karan to go around the building and attack the guard from the other side. Once Karan got around and was ready, Zia threw a stone to distract the guard, which forced the guard to walk out, into the passage. Karan pounced on him and knocked him out with the butt of his gun. Zia and Karan quietly walked in again. There was a flight of descending stairs that took them a level down. Zia was wondering if it was the right way but then she saw another man right outside another door. This guy had a gun in his hand. 'Are these guys really guards or have they been placed out here to show us the way!' Zia couldn't even laugh at her own joke. Her heart was galloping and her limbs were beginning to go numb. They were right at the middle of the action and anything could happen.

Zia pulled out the silencer barrel and slowly attached it to her pistol, trying to take cover and not expose herself. With bated breath, she took aim at the guard at the door from a dark corner about 20 metres away and fired. There was a soft sound despite the silencer, but not loud enough to sound an alarm. The man at the door who was shot at, took a few steps with resurgence and pulled out a gun himself, before falling flat on the ground.

Zia immediately alerted her team that was waiting outside and asked them to track her location and come inside.

Karan and she took the stairs down and went in through the door. Everything was pitch dark inside the door and they had no idea as to where they were. Zia stumbled onto something and fell to the floor. She pulled out her phone and switched on the torch. They were in an empty room. There was no other door, other than what they had come through. Zia had stumbled on what looked like a handle to a lid. She tried lifting the lid, it didn't give in easily. Together they tried pulling the lid out, it didn't move an inch. They then tried the reverse and tried to push it in, the lid started giving in. They pushed so hard that the lid went in completely and they both fell into a cellar.

What Zia saw next completely shocked her. They were in a massive hall that was brightly lit, with a lot of well-defined areas and tables. There was a massive table in the centre, which had a mountain of small packets. Small packets of cocaine which were yellow in colour. Those that were being referred to as the "Golden Snow". There were heaps and heaps of it. On one end of the hall was an area with another table. Near the table, there were refrigerated cocoa leaves and on the table were cutting and grinding instruments. On the next table were a lot of chemicals, and the table and that area itself resembled a chemistry lab. The next table was set up with packaging materials and wrappers.

On the other end of the hall there was a small room with glass walls. Inside the room was Dr Craig Langer, the leading pharmacologist, sitting and studying the samples and scribbling something in his notebook.

On either side of the hall were doors opening onto passages. They could see nobody else in the hall other than Dr Langer who was working inside the glass room.

'Holy fuck! These rogues are running a cocaine factory here,' Zia remarked in utter disbelief and astonishment, still unable to overcome what she had seen.

Karan was suddenly ambushed from behind. He was held firmly and his head was slammed repeatedly on the table. It was Billu. He kicked aside Karan and was walking towards Zia.

Zia pulled out her gun and pinned him down. By then her team had arrived.

∞

As Tony had said before the match, the Dragons were a batsman short. None of them made a big score but each one fought well. Fought as if their entire life depended on that final. Vinayak was the top scorer with 40 runs. Nikhil made 35, Pranav made 25, Tony 22 and Tushar made 15. The Dragons somehow managed to put 137 runs on the board. The Titans needed 138 runs to win the final.

'138 runs in this pitch should be a walk in the park for the Titans, especially with Ritesh and Amay in such good form,' said the commentators on air, as Ritesh and Amay strode out to the middle.

'I'm telling you again, if the main bowlers are hit, you grab that ball and bowl.' These were Vivank's last words to Tony before the team went in. On the giant screen, he saw Leepa praying, sitting on the wheel chair, as Irfan took his huge strides and ran on to bowl the first over.

'Bowled them,' cried the commentators on air and the stadium erupted, as Amay's stumps were uprooted by Irfan's very first ball and were lying somewhere near the wicket keeper. Amay stood his ground in utter disbelief and then slowly walked back to the pavilion.

Irfan had the Titans on the mat claiming three wickets in no time. The pace and bounce that Irfan was generating was something unheard of in the Mumbai domestic circuit and the national player Ritesh was in all sorts of trouble dealing with Irfan. But Ritesh was experienced enough to play out Irfan and stay alive at the crease.

Rohan and Vineet tried to keep up the pressure but the scoreboard was ticking as long as Ritesh was at the crease. The Titans were 68/5 at the half way mark. They needed 70 runs off the last 60 balls and Ritesh decided to really go after Rajawat. The Titans plundered away the next 40 runs in no time. Rajawat was taken to the cleaners. Vivank was kicking himself as to why Tony was not bowling. He tried sending out messages to Tony, but in vain. Tony brought Irfan for one final over, much earlier than they had planned to, with the hope of getting a wicket, preferably that of Ritesh. Irfan bowled a tight over but couldn't get a wicket.

Sixteen runs were needed off the last two overs and the Titans had four wickets in hand.

During the time out, Tony told Vivank that he wasn't confident of his own bowling.

'Rohan will bowl the 19th and Vineet will bowl the last,' he told Vivank.

'Only 16 runs are needed. The only way we win this is by

getting wickets. Rajawat will still bowl the 19th and you will bowl the 20th. This is my final word,' Vivank spoke sternly.

'When you bowl the last over, you will bowl the back of length cutters that we have been practising,' he added.

Tony just nodded and went in.

Rajawat came on to bowl the penultimate over. He was completely a new bowler, but knew that his captain and coach were fully backing him. He flighted and spun the ball boldly ending up with two crucial wickets in that over, but he also gave away eight runs off that over.

'Eight runs needed off the last over with two wickets left. The Titans are still the favourites to win this, especially with Ritesh still on the crease. Will Ritesh finish it off with a six at the Wankhede, just like the great Dhoni?' remarked the excited commentators.

'Will it be Vineet or Rohan?' Was the question on everybody's mind.

'Oh boy! Dragons captain Tony has grabbed the ball from the umpire and is marking his run up. This is out of the box. What a night! What a final!' the commentators were jumping with excitement.

Ritesh got ready to face at the strikers end as Tony got ready to bowl. Tony briefly looked at Vivank who was repeatedly signalling him. Vivank was hitting his palms with the other hand placed vertically, which was their signal for a back of a length cutter. Vivank clearly anticipated Ritesh to come down the track and hit Tony straight back over his head. So, he wanted to pull back the length a bit in the last possible moment and deliver a slower bowl.

Tony ran and was in his delivery stride, Ritesh stepped out of his crease and brought his bat straight out. Tony held back his length and bowled the slow cutter. The ball was slightly out of

Ritesh's reach, he still went ahead and completed his shot, resulting in the ball hitting the top edge of the bat and going up in the air. The ball didn't have the distance and soon landed in Tony's own hands. Ritesh exchanged a few words with Tony before leaving the ground in a furious mood. Vivank pumping his fist in the dressing room and hugged Cheeku.

'Master stroke!' patted an emotional Cheeku, not letting go of the hug.

The last batsman for the Titans walked in. Still, eight runs were needed off five deliveries. The batsman was beaten off the first ball.

Now eight runs needed off four balls. Tony ran and bowled another cutter, this time a fuller length. The batsman swung his bat and missed. The ball clipped the bails that gently fell. The entire stadium erupted. The Dragons had won the MSL. Tony removed his shirt and went into a wild celebration with his team mates. Then entire team started running towards Vivank. Leepa and Pravi hugged each other. Leepa was in uncontrollable tears. Cheeku was running around Instagramming the moments. Vivank sunk his face into his hands and sat on a chair. The greatest night of his life was smiling upon him!

※

'Dr Langer and Billu have been arrested. All the materials have been seized, sir,' Zia diligently reported everything to the head of her department, the director general of police.

'No sir, we haven't found MM yet but we will find him soon sir,' she hung up. She was traveling back to the city after completing her operation successfully.

She then got a call from Himanshu.

'Ma'am, you are great, ma'am. But I'm still not able to make sense of a few things. Why did they set it up at that place ma'am?' asked Himanshu.

'The soil at the ocean cliff is filled with unique variants of calcareous and siliceous oozes, which have been formed by the skeletal remains of microscopic organisms and various dumps at the harbour that feed into this soil. Over the years, the deposition has led to the formation of a mineral that produces a chemical called calcitate. It is this mineral, which could produce calcitate that they are all interested in,' explained Zia.

'Why would they want this mineral, ma'am?'

'This is where Dr Langer comes in. He has done extensive research on the pharmacokinetic properties of calcitate. He has set up his lab at the cellar to convert the precursor mineral into calcitate. This mineral is not of much use and not valuable either, which is why no government or a private entity took any interest in this so far. But this calcitate, rightly combined with cocaine and cooked well, produces the distinct yellow powder, which is now known as the Golden Snow. This Golden Snow is twenty times more powerful than regular cocaine,' Zia further added.

'Oh my god. I'm beginning to understand, ma'am, this is beyond reality,' exclaimed Himanshu.

'Yes. Dr Langer and Anand were friends since the time Anand was in the armed forces. Anand had deliberately walked out of the forces feigning ill health to set up a small cocaine supply chain with the help of Dr Langer. Initially, he used his travel agency as the drug laundry point but later as his business grew, stepped up into the Swamiji avatar. Soon his market grew and so did his popularity and influence. He soon discovered the calcitate deposits near the cliff and Langer confirmed the existence of the precursor mineral here. He then made the blue print for the biggest drug factory in

India. The place for the factory was readily available in close vicinity to the secluded cliff—it was the RKM school. When he tried to buy out the school, he couldn't succeed. The school belonged to one Mr Laxman, a member of the Mumbai Cricket Association who had no intention of selling the school. Anand also needed an experienced hand to deal with the backend of his operations and productions. He met MM in Arthur Road jail and lured him into his plan. Given the image of "Swamiji" and the kind of influence he had by then and the profitability of Golden Snow, MM didn't waste any time to join hands with him. Then Swamiji got MM to buy the cricket team along with the school aka their prospective cocaine factory. Mr Laxman, who was a devoted cricket enthusiast, sold off his school in the interest of getting a new cricket ground and development of cricket in the region,'

Zia elaborated.

'I can't even believe what I am hearing, ma'am. This is beyond fiction. MM bought this team to get access to this ground, where he could set up his underground cocaine factory. He could easily source the precursor mineral and Dr Langer would synthesize calcitate out of it and produce golden snow! The cricket team was just a sham. Oh my god!' Himanshu breathing heavily.

'And they have also constructed a tunnel from their cellar hall right into the heart of rock cliff,' Zia further added information.

'You're truly a genius ma'am; how you got to the bottom of it all?' Himanshu couldn't control his appreciation for Zia.

'To have the cricket team by their side, they must be minting a lot of money out of this, ma'am?' Himanshu asked curiously.

'Yes. A lot of money. To maximize profits, cocaine producers use cutting agents like caffeine, creatinine, sometimes even laundry detergents in the ratio of 1:1 per cocaine cake. This increases the volume. However, in case of Golden Snow, our forensic sample reports show no such cutting agent but only pure calcitate. This amplifies the effect by about twenty times. They purchased huge amounts of cocoa leaves from Femi and his friends, which came via the sea. MM would have easily made about ₹10 crore per day!' Zia added.

'And the entire team cost him only ₹5 crore! ₹6 crore with the school! What a businessman,' Himanshu exclaimed.

'You call that business, Himanshu. Seriously?!'

'No ma'am, I was too excited,' confessed Himanshu.

'Call for a press conference with the same excitement, I'll be reaching office in an hour,' Zia ordered.

CHAPTER 18

Hot Pursuit

Vivank couldn't sleep that night. It was past midnight and was drizzling outside. He was in the comfort of his flat, sitting on his favourite sofa. Vivank was slowly letting that wonderful feeling sink in. In front of him was the MSL trophy, which all the players respectfully presented him with. Leepa was lying on the sofa with her head on his lap getting sound sleep after a very long time. Vivank was playing with her hair, reliving the best moments of the night from the Wankhede Stadium.

Cheeku was sitting near him and was following every tweet and post about MSL. He suddenly came running to Vivank.

'See this! Tariq has posted a congratulatory message to the team,' he showed his phone excitedly.

'That's nice. At least he isn't harbouring any negative feelings,' Vivank said.

'Only you think like this. Since the last game he has been extremely sarcastic about our team. His last tweet today was at the half way mark during the second innings. He trolled us for not having a genuine experienced player to fall back on. He followed it with a picture of him happily sitting at home and enjoying watching us lose. He had just one hashtag for that picture—

#Happiness!' Cheeku put forth all his deductions.

'Is it? And he is congratulating us now?' asked Vivank.

'Yes. He has deleted all his previous posts!' explained Cheeku.

'Oh!'

'Of which I have screenshots!' Cheeku laughed cheekily.

'Did you see the news about the drug racket that DC Zia has busted?' Cheeku asked Vivank.

'Yeah briefly, while changing channels. Didn't like the topic, so didn't watch much,' Vivank replied.

'They have linked it to our team owners,' Cheeku added.

'Oh dear! I didn't know this!' Vivank switched on the TV.

As expected, the news about Golden Snow was all over the television channels.

'Holy crap! They have been using our ground for making this hybrid coke! Right under our noses!' exclaimed Cheeku.

'Yeah!'

'What do you mean by yeah?' asked Cheeku

'Meaning I didn't know earlier.' Vivank tried to explain.

'That's seriously amusing!' Cheeku couldn't control his laughter, he kept laughing until Vivank threw a few things that were within his reach at him.

A press release was issued by Pravi—chairman and managing director of Dongri Dragons Cricket Ltd—that was being flashed on TV news.

The release said that the ownership of the DDCL was vested with her and the management had nothing to do with all the untoward incidents that were happening.

Vivank immediately called Pravi, who assured him that she was at the helm of things and the team wasn't in any danger.

'That's good to hear but I'm worried that the team management will be under scanner and be subject to investigation,' Vivank said.

'Don't worry. I'm prepared for it and for legal remediation. We built this champion team and it will always be with us,' Pravi said.

∽

'Search the entire house, every single inch,' Zia ordered as her jeep arrived at the port.

'We have searched everywhere, ma'am. Except the glass cage. Nothing suspicious found. We have gone through all the papers that we laid our hands on,' reported the inspector who was heading the search.

'Do you need a special invitation to search the glass cage? Go and search, I tell you!'

'Ma'am...ma'am! I don't think we can search the glass cage!'

'What is it, you idiot? Is there a snake inside hissing loudly that you can't search?'

'Yes, ma'am. There's a snake really. A huge python!'

'What! This MM doesn't cease to surprise me! Call some snake charmer, clear it and search!'

By the time she finished this call, Karan was on the other line.

'Ma'am all roads out of Mumbai have been sealed. All the airlines and private jet operators have been intimated. MM cannot leave the city now,' said Karan.

'That is all fine but MM always prefers the sea. If my guess is right, he would have already taken the sea route,' Zia spoke in a sharp tone.

Suddenly there was a voice on the mic.

'Ma'am, MM hasn't been seen near the regular port area or the gateway area,' informed one of her men.

'What about Vasai?' Zia asked.

'No ma'am, our men are there too.'

'Have you informed the coast guards?'

'Yes, ma'am.'

'Let me know once you get some info,' Zia ordered.

By the time she hung up there was another call. Zia picked immediately.

'Holy shit! He has dared to take the rock cliff route and has escaped in his fishing yacht! This is insane! He knew the place was sealed and our people are thinning out there and got away! Rascal!' Zia shouted angrily.

'Okay then. It's gonna end like it began. Another bloody shootout in the middle of the sea!' Zia was breathing heavily as she uttered the words.

She immediately called her standby team and told them to get a speed boat to Eagle Point, which was midway between the main port and rock cliff.

'Eagle Point…immediately,' she cried. She just had four men with her including the driver. She pulled all the ammunition she could possibly carry from her vehicle and loaded her waterproof bag. Anticipating MM would take the sea, she also had her diving suit ready.

They soon reached Eagle Point, and Zia got onto their speed boat with the four men she had with her. They zoomed into the sea, in hot pursuit of MM's yacht.

'He wouldn't dare to cross the international borders so just keep going northeast,' she instructed her man who was steering the boat.

After some time, they spotted a yacht, about 500–600 metres away.

'There are four of them, ma'am. May be a few more inside,'

said her guy who was watching through the binoculars.

Zia got the binoculars from him and had a look. She couldn't find MM. But she saw Ricky. Standing on the other side with a gun in one hand and a cricket bat in the other hand. Few other men were also armed.

'Are you sure you saw MM?' Zia asked.

'Yes, ma'am,' reverted her men.

'Okay, let me dive and go in, if you don't get any instructions from me for more than 30 mins, attack the yacht,' Zia gave one final set of instructions to her team and jumped in.

All her recent injuries made swimming extremely difficult for her.

'Should I have opened fire from the boat itself?' she was thinking as she got to the yacht.

It was almost dark as she climbed onto the back of the yacht and sneaked in.

'Thud!' came a huge noise from behind as Zia entered the yacht. She was slapped right at the back of her head with the cricket bat that Ricky had been holding not long ago. MM walked in proudly in front of her, with the cricket bat still in his hand, like a batsman who had just hit a six.

It was so painful that Zia couldn't even shout, all she knew was MM had hit her from behind; she collapsed right into her own pool of blood. She didn't even know if she would survive or if this was her last breath.

※

Zia could barely open her eyes. She was still lying in the same place. Fortunately for her, the bleeding had stopped. But the pain was just insane. She felt numb with pain. She didn't even have the strength to lift her arm or shout for help, let alone get up and fight again. She tried looking around and saw her men lying dead in front of her.

'Ah! Finally, the princess has a woken. Just wanted you to wake up and look into my eyes when I shoot you down! Classic finish!' said MM.

'Oye Ricky! Throw me the gun. I will finish her,' called out MM.

Ricky threw the gun to him immediately, as he always did diligently.

'Here we go Madame Zia, one…two…three…' MM gave his most satisfying laugh and pulled the trigger on Zia.

Nothing happened.

'Oye Ricky! This is not working. Give me another gun,' shouted MM.

Ricky pulled out another gun from his back. Instead of throwing it to MM, he started talking aloud in a thunderous voice.

'Rishikesh Kishan, IPS aka Ricky!' He said, with his most satisfying laugh, looking into MM's horrified eyes.

The images of all the crimes MM committed and the innocent lives that he claimed flashed across Ricky's mind one after the other. That image of MM making him run down Zia with his car made him blind with rage.

Without speaking another word, Ricky pulled the trigger, tearing MM apart with his bullets.

He then pulled out his phone and called his boss at the police department.

'MM is down sir, but the mission not yet accomplished. Anand Bhatia is believed to be on a cruise ship called the *Aqua Dream* to Southeast Asia. I can reach the cruise ship in a couple of hours, but I will need all the clearances to enter, sir,' Ricky informed his boss on the phone.

'Wonderful Ricky! That is why you are one of our department's best! I'll get all your clearances right away,' came the voice from the other end.

'And by the way, Zia is alive, sir, but she is grievously hurt and will be needing an emergency medical team to rescue her,' Ricky added.

∽

'Hi Mr Anand Bhatia. Oh! Sorry Col Anand Bhatia. Nice to meet you,' Ricky was inside the *Aqua Dream*.

His undercover mission along with a few of his trusted colleagues from the police department had started a few years ago to wipe out the entire drug network of Mumbai. Their primary target was MM, and as Ricky went about his mission surrounding MM and his accomplices, he realised the magnitude of the situation and the massive number of deadly people involved in the network. He began tracking down everything, pretending to be MM's accomplice. He eventually won MM's trust and passed on vital information to his department and to Zia, who was like his female version but on regular duty. He came close to killing MM on quite a few occasions, especially when he hurt Zia, but somehow restrained himself looking at the larger picture and how this colonel was planning something much bigger with MM's help.

MM was particularly secretive about the colonel aka Swamiji. It was only a few hours before he had alerted Zia and she rushed to RKM School that Ricky came to know about the functioning secret cocaine lab at the school.

And now he was on the verge of completing his mission. MM was done. Dr Langer and Billu were already arrested. So were the second level dealers operating in the network. Now, he had reached the brainchild behind this big game. Ricky knew that this was the crucial step of the mission. To deactivate the brain.

Anand Bhatia aka colonel aka Swamiji was a strong, 50-year-old, 6-feet-tall man with a typically long 'Swamiji' like grey beard. He had long grey hair, which he had tied with a band and wore modern designer clothes and looked part of the tourist crowd on the ship.

'What a big scoundrel you are Mr Bhatia,' Ricky came straight to the point, looking squarely into his eyes. Colonel was watching television in the lounge sipping away at a glass of martini.

By then he had received the information that MM had been taken down. MM was originally supposed to join him on the ship and they were planning to escape to Palawan.

But now, given MM was down, he knew that they would come for him next. His only hope was time and thought he could make a narrow escape before the police figured out where he was, as only MM knew his location. Little did he know that Ricky was an undercover agent and was with MM when he told the colonel that he would reach the *Aqua Dream* in a few hours.

But now he knew and realised that it was over.

'Arrey all of us are scoundrels in this world, bhai. Look at you for example. Didn't you play imposter? Is it not cheating? Is it not a sin? People of this world are born to commit sins; it is in all our karma. To commit sins,' he spoke with his characteristic pause in between words.

'Keep all of this for your stages and YouTube,' Ricky cut him short.

'People loved me for my honesty. I'm honest about myself and about everyone in this world. Which is why I am what I am today. I'm an asset to our country. Do you know how much forex

I generate for India?' the colonel asked.

'We will sit and calculate that in jail. And as for your reach, we will see your reach once I share your arrest video on YouTube,' retorted Ricky.

'You know what? Arrest is one of the cruellest things in this world. Man is not an animal. Man is born free and he is...'

Ricky gave him a tight slap, handcuffed him and took him away.

CHAPTER 19

Reunion 2.0

A few months later
Blue Paradise Beach Resort, Goa

It was a bright morning in Panjim. The sun was shining brightly and a gentle, cool breeze was blowing. The water was sparkling around the beach, where clusters of beach beds were laid out in a symmetrical fashion at a stone's throw from the waves.

Vivank and Leepa had just gotten married and were cuddling on one bed, chuckling, laughing and telling foolish jokes to each other.

Zia walked in, in an ice blue swimsuit, and set her beach bed up, adjoining to Vivank and Leepa.

'Oh! I never thought you would wear swimwear,' remarked Vivank, getting a playful slap from Leepa for the comment.

'Yeah! I do wear swimwear. But only when my husband is around,' remarked Zia with a bashful smile.

In walked Ricky wearing navy blue swimming shorts and a wayfarers applying sunscreen across his face.

He pulled a beach bed close to Zia, sat down and put his arm around Zia.

'Yeah, put your arm around me now, run me over with cars later!' Zia complained and tried to take his hand out.

Ricky laughed. 'How many times have I told you? It could have been worse had MM been the one driving the car, I tried to be as gentle as possible with only a "leg break"!' he continued.

'What a leg break. Rajawat would be proud of it!' joined Vivank.

Zia gave Vivank a stern look and continued.

'And you allowed me to get thrashed with a cricket bat! You fool! What sort of a husband are you?'

'Err…Well…That was pretty bad timing. I knew you had jumped from your boat. I thought I will finish off others in my boat before you came. Slight miss in the timing baby!'

'Ya, slight miss in the timing. I would have died and you would have shamelessly been on your second honeymoon by now.'

'But you could have finished off MM earlier?' Vivank asked curiously.

'I could have. I had instructions to wait until everything about Golden Snow was out in the open and the colonel was captured. By the end it became too personal and I got to finish him off in front of her. Anyways all is well now,' Ricky said.

'Nice finish brother,' Vivank said cheekily.

'See, I also helped you as much as I could. I got to Dr Langer's documents before you, and I shared it all with you, helped you spot Rathod, helped you track Femi, sent you details about the cocaine lab. I also sent you the last location coordinates of MM's yacht! So much I have helped you in this case. Accept it,' Ricky tried to level his scores.

'Hmm…okay, fine whatever! Be done with all your undercover things with this. I'm tired of telling the neighbours that my boyfriend ran away. I'm even more tired of having just Candy Crush for company. No more undercover and secret meetings. Only regular work for you henceforth,' Zia told clearly.

'Yeah, yeah. I too want a break. Vivank and I are starting a cricket academy soon,' Ricky said.

Soon all four were chatting and sipping away mocktails. Just then one of the hotel staff came up to them.

'I was given a note for you, sir' he told Ricky.

'By whom?' Ricky asked.

'We don't know, sir. The note was delivered via courier with no sender address.'

Ricky opened it and stared at the bold, black letters.

'Your end begins now!'